One Step
AHEAD

One Step AHEAD

a novel by

M.C. Millman

The Judaica Press, Inc.

ISBN: 978-1-60763-268-9 (softcover ed.)
        1-932443-16-5 (hardcover ed.)

Cover design & typography by: Zisi Berkowitz
Editor: Bonnie Goldman

Other books by M.C. Millman

Juggling Act
Locked in Time

THE JUDAICA PRESS, INC.
718-972-6200   800-972-6201
info@judaicapress.com
www.judaicapress.com

Manufactured in the United States of America

ONE

Shira took one last look around her apartment to make sure there wasn't anything left from the mound of items to pack. The pile had been building steadily ever since she had accepted this job. As she looked around, Shira's green eyes caught her reflection in the bedroom mirror.

"Good luck!" she mouthed to her openly staring mirror image. "You're going to need it!"

She reached up to smooth a loose strand of her shoulder-length, sandy brown hair. After affirming that all was well with her carefully made-up face, Shira swung her hair slightly and watched it settle with a satisfying swirl as it reformed, meeting in the back in a perfect layered "V."

What was she getting herself into? But then she steeled herself. It was necessary. It was even essential. It had all been explained to her, and it all made sense.

She wasn't sure that all those involved would agree, but this was just too big of an issue to consider what the little people thought. She had a job she had agreed to do, a job that was too important for her to let minor things like her emotions, or her guilt feelings of what might be right or wrong get in the way.

Success was vital. Failure was not even a word that could flicker through her conscience.

Shira had to succeed. She would make it up to everyone somehow if she had to answer for the deception, but later, much later. For now, there was only the inevitable—days and weeks of planning and plotting and scheming. Days and weeks of pretending to be someone that she wasn't. She knew she could do it. She was the best woman for the job, or she would never have accepted in the first place. She would succeed, because success was paramount.

TWO

"A *babysitter!*" Simcha exclaimed in disgust. "But that's for babies."

The three Eisenberg children had been called into their father's bedroom for an informal family conference of some sort. The cool air from the air conditioning vent blew gently on Simcha where he had positioned himself against the wall. Summer had struck full force as soon as school had let out, and hadn't let up since, and Simcha preferred the cool air to the already heated atmosphere in the bedroom.

"Right," said Binyamin Eisenberg, trying not to get flustered before he had even started. "I meant a sitter not a *baby* sitter. Of course, you're much too big for a *baby* sitter."

"Word games," muttered Menucha, equally miffed with her father's news.

"Yeah, same difference," said Simcha as he stuffed his hands deeper into his pockets.

Their mere eighteen-month age difference made them perfectly understanding of each other at times like this.

"Whatever you want to call her," their father said, deciding that the best way to handle two teenagers was to be firm, "she'll be here tomorrow because I have to leave."

"She!" said Simcha, latching onto the next thing to complain about with all the vehemence a thirteen-year-old boy could muster. "Why does it always have to be a *she* that watches us? Can't you get a *he* for once?"

"No," said Binyamin firmly, deciding that that was the best track to take. The direction of this conversation was going anywhere but the way he had planned. "The sitter is going to be a lady. She works for the company, and I expect you all to behave *exactly* as if I was here watching you."

"How long?" Yocheved asked as she rubbed her thumb nervously across her upper lip while holding a twist of her long, dark hair in her hand.

Simcha teased his little sister mercilessly whenever he caught her sucking her thumb. Seven was much too big to still be sucking her thumb, he told her time and time again. Though he could tell she wanted to suck her thumb desperately right now, his close proximity was enough of an incentive to stop her now.

"I'm not really sure," said Binyamin, as he reached over to draw his youngest onto his lap. "It might be only a week or it might be longer. It really depends on how quickly I'm able to find the materials I need for the business."

"What are you going for this time?" asked Simcha, showing a grudging interest.

His father's business trips, made a few times a year, always fascinated Simcha.

"Water pearls mostly, although I might pick up some other stones," said Binyamin casually.

Yocheved's thumb wandered up to finger her freshwater pearl earrings given to her by her father. She had absolutely no idea how valuable the one-of-a-kind, specially designed pearl and tri-colored gold twist earrings were. At seven years old she was used to fine jewelry. Her father had been showering her with it since she was a tiny baby, and then later to try to make up to her for the foul blow life had dealt her. She and her brother and sister had lost their mother four years ago, when Yocheved was only three.

"We have a whole new line of ingenious new designs that we're bringing out soon," her father continued. "Now that I have these amazing new designs, I have to find a supplier with the quality we need to take the market by storm. I know who has the supply, but I just don't know if he wants to deal with us. Bi Hai Shan is quite exclusive, and has to be handled just so. He doesn't like to take on new customers."

"Who?" Yocheved asked, smiling at the strange sounding name.

"Never mind," her father said, holding her tight. "I'll bring you back something special. You two think about what you might want. Yocheved is going to get a silk kimono and a bracelet to match the one that's too small for her now."

"Baila Chana wears it now," said Yocheved, fondly fingering the shiny, gold chain bracelet, oblivious to the fact that her favorite doll was being adorned in jewels worth far more than the doll's value. "We can be twins."

"You can't be twins," said Simcha heartlessly. "She's not your age or your size, and she's not even real."

"Simcha," said his father in his warning tone as he noticed Yocheved's eyes filling with tears. "Don't cry, honey. Did I tell you the best thing of all?"

"What, Tatti?" Yocheved asked brightly, her tears suddenly forgotten.

"I'm also going to give all of my girls the first pieces of jewelry off of the new line. We'll be producing them at the end of this summer, after I purchase the water pearls that I need."

"What's it going to look like?" Menucha asked.

"Hand me the file over there," her father instructed.

Menucha went over to the dresser and brought the leather zip-up file to her father's bed. He unzipped the file case and shuffled through the pages.

"It's at times like this," muttered Simcha, "that I wonder if it's really worth being a boy."

"I'll make it worth your while," said his father with a laugh. "You'll see when I get back from China, but for now, how about this?" he asked his daughters as they leaned in to study a sketch of a water pearl bracelet with a unique design of swirls of dangling pearls on a patterned and etched gold chain.

"I like those," Yocheved said, pointing to the matching earrings.

"They're too old for you," Menucha said.

"Tatti said they're new," protested Yocheved, "not old."

"How about this?" her father asked, showing her a different page with a similar design but a simpler pattern. "These designs were all made by a new designer. Aren't they something else?"

"They're all so pretty," said Yocheved. "How will I pick one? Can I decide later which one I want?"

"You can look it over and let me know after I get back," said her father, giving her a squeeze. "All right, I have to get back to packing, and I have to print up a bunch of stuff so I can leave you guys with phone numbers and other instructions just in case."

"In case of what?" asked Yocheved, looking up from the folder of designs she was still closely scrutinizing.

"In case this babysitter turns out to be like the last one," said Simcha.

"Yeah," said Menucha, remembering that one. "She worked for you, too, and you thought she was perfect."

"She was perfect for work," admitted their father with a sigh, as he wearily rubbed his fingers through his short salt and pepper hair.

"But she wasn't too good as a sitter," said Menucha. "If you would just let *me* take care of everyone like I do every day, we wouldn't even need a sitter!"

"You're fifteen years old, Menucha," Binyamin said. "No one goes away and leaves a fifteen year old in charge of things."

"I don't see why not," Menucha huffed. "I do a perfectly good job of it every day as it is."

"Yes, you do, Menucha," said her father. "You're wonderful, but that's when I'm right here. My office is only one phone call and three minutes away."

"And you can cook," said Simcha. "Remember that last sitter?"

"She couldn't cook worth beans," said Menucha, "and she wouldn't let me near the kitchen either."

"She thought you were too young," Simcha said. "We had pizza or take-out every night until Tatti came home."

"Remember all that laundry she left you?" Yocheved added.

"She wouldn't let me near the machine," said a disgruntled Menucha.

"And do you remember how messy the house was?" Yocheved said.

"I wasn't allowed to touch the vacuum," Menucha said loftily.

"And how we ran out of fruit and cereal?" Simcha said.

"At least you were all watched over," Binyamin said weakly, looking at his kids a little helplessly.

"Right," said Simcha, "if you want to call it that."

"We don't need any *baby* sitter. We're not babies," Menucha said with the confident air of an eldest. "I still say that I could do a better job myself."

"Sorry," said her father. "Maybe one day. But not now."

"I hope this person is better than your last choice is all I can say," said Simcha.

"Oh, she is," said Binyamin quickly. "I've checked her out really well."

"That's what you said last time," said Menucha ominously.

"I'm not worried," their father said, determined not to be swayed by his rather persuasive children. He got up to begin packing and consulting the multitude of lists he kept stored in his electronic pocket organizer.

All three of the kids trailed mournfully behind. They hated when their father left them, no matter what amazing gifts he promised to return with.

THREE

Binyamin stared at his open suitcase, his eyes unseeing as he mulled through the torrent of thoughts rushing through his head. He reached for his organizer and entered another half dozen last-minute items onto his packing list. Then he switched screens on the organizer and added another few notes for the sitter, and switched to another screen to add yet another emergency contact just in case all of the other ones he had provided proved unavailable. Of course, he planned to have his cell phone turned on at all times, but you could never really rely on a cell phone, especially given the large distance that would be separating him from his children. He paused, remembering that he would have to add his cell phone number to the list, but since it was a new cell phone with a satellite connection (so that it would work even from China), he had to go look up the number.

Binyamin could hear crickets chirping as he went to his dresser to pack his socks. He couldn't help but smile at the tidy sections of his sock drawer, neatly organized and compartmentalized by color and style, compliments of Menucha, who felt it was her job to be the substitute mother of all occupants in the house. He certainly hoped the sitter would be able to harness Menucha's greatest attributes—her willingness to help in all areas around the house. And he hoped she would not discover the strong animosity that Menucha felt towards her unknown sitter, who simply by dint of her being present was stepping on the fifteen-year-old's toes.

It was important for the sitter to win Menucha over if she was going to be successful at running the house peacefully. As for the other two, Binyamin knew it wouldn't be too hard to get on their good sides, but Menucha was different. This was her house, her territory, and any other female stepping in was stepping on Menucha as well. It didn't have to be that way, Binyamin knew. It wasn't right for it to be that way either, but that was Menucha for you. For all of Menucha's good qualities, among them her fierce feelings of love and protection for her siblings and home, the result was that she didn't like anyone to step over the line into what she viewed as her domain.

He wished this sitter every bit of luck. She was going to need it if she was going to succeed. And Binyamin needed her to succeed, for the sake of the whole family.

FOUR

"So what do you think?" Menucha asked, looking her brother straight in the eye.

It wasn't hard to do. Despite her being eighteen months older, they were exactly the same height.

"I think she's nice enough," said Simcha with a shrug.

"She's so pretty," breathed Yocheved.

"Pretty has nothing to do with it," said Menucha, "not if we're going to be stuck with her taking care of us until Tatti gets back."

"Her hair is so shiny," said Yocheved again.

"Leave it to a seven-year-old to judge how nice her babysitter is by how shiny her hair is," said Menucha with a sniff. "Your hair is just as shiny, Yocheved. I make sure of that."

"I know," said Yocheved, backing a few steps away from her

sister just in case Menucha got any bright ideas about brushing out Yocheved's long, straight, dark hair, something that Menucha already did far too frequently for Yocheved's taste.

"Anyway," said Menucha, "Tatti is just showing her around the house before he leaves. I say there's something strange about her is all."

"She *just* got here," said Simcha, looking at his sister with some exasperation. "What could possibly be strange about her walking in the house when Tatti opened the door for her, which is about all you've seen of her anyway?"

"Oh, I don't know," said Menucha. "It's just a feeling. Did you see the way she looked at each of us when she looked up and saw us here on the stair landing? It was like she was measuring us to see if we fit."

"Fit what?" asked Simcha.

"For presents she brought us?" suggested Yocheved hopefully, looking up from her doll, Baila Chana, whose outfit she was changing so she would be prepared to meet the new sitter.

"She's our babysitter," said Simcha in disgust, "not some vis- iting relative, though she looks about as old as Tatti's sister. She won't have brought us presents."

"Oh," said Yocheved, sounding disappointed.

"And you're just jealous, Menucha," said Simcha. "You get like this every time we have a sitter. Face it, you're just not old enough to take care of us and the house on your own."

"I am perfectly capable of—" Menucha spluttered indignantly.

"No one's saying you're not *capable* of it," Simcha interrupted. "It's just that you're too young."

"Too young!" said Menucha. "That is *so* unfair!"

"I know," said Yocheved, nodding in perfect empathy. "I'm always too young, too."

"You know what I think," said Menucha. "I thi—"

"—Menucha, Simcha, Yocheved," their father's voice called them from the landing of the steps where they had been busily conferring. "Come and say goodbye. I'm going to leave as soon as the taxi arrives."

The children thundered down the stairs to say goodbye to their father, but first there were introductions all around.

"So this is Yocheved," the babysitter said, kneeling down so that she could look eye to eye with the youngest Eisenberg. "I've been looking forward to meeting you for ever so long. We are going to have so much fun together. And this must be Baila Chana."

"You *know* Baila Chana?" Yocheved asked, looking down with surprise at the life-size doll she clutched.

"Of course I know all about Baila Chana," the babysitter said with some satisfaction. "Your father told me that she wears all the old clothes you used to wear when you were six months old."

"You talked about dolls with my father?" asked Simcha, looking up at his father in disgust.

"Among other things," said Mr. Eisenberg hastily, a brown carry-on bag now slung over his shoulder as his other hand gripped the extended handle of his large, navy blue suitcase. "Anyway, I have that plane to catch. Shira, this is Simcha, and this is—"

"Menucha," she said, smiling at the three of them. "I know

we're all going to get along great!" She then turned to Mr. Eisenberg. "You have a safe trip! I'll take care of everything here."

"Don't bet on it," muttered Menucha.

"What was that, Menucha?" Mr. Eisenberg said sharply as he turned to face Menucha.

"Nothing," said Menucha sulking.

"I didn't think so," said Mr. Eisenberg. "I know you are all going to behave perfectly."

"Baila Chana, too," said Yocheved, looking with glowing eyes at the new babysitter.

Recognition of her favorite doll meant a lot to Yocheved. The sitter had chalked up high points with at least one of the Eisenbergs.

"There's the cab," Menucha said, as the honking could be heard long before the cab had even turned into their driveway.

"I'll see you all real soon," said Mr. Eisenberg, reaching out to encircle his children in a tremendous bear hug. "Be good. I'll miss you!"

"Come home soon, Tatti," lisped Yocheved from around the thumb that had slipped into her mouth unnoticed by her and her brother.

"Have a safe trip," said the sitter, as the four of them trooped out onto the porch, waving frantically as Mr. Eisenberg walked to the cab.

As their father climbed into the cab, Yocheved promptly burst into tears. Menucha, used to mothering her baby sister, drew Yocheved close, patting her back until the racking sobs subsided.

All the while, the babysitter looked on, with a smile that

seemed to sag with relief once the hugs and the goodbyes were all over, once Mr. Eisenberg was safely ensconced, luggage and all, in the fast disappearing taxi, leaving the children alone with a babysitter they had only just met: Shira Baum.

FIVE

"Excuse me," Binyamin Eisenberg said politely to a young man sitting in an aisle seat. "I believe I'm sitting in the seat next to you."

The young man languidly moved his legs in slightly towards his seat, all the while staring pointedly at Binyamin's yarmulke. Binyamin was hard pressed not to stare himself. From the blond hair pulled back in a greasy ponytail, to the large rips in both knees of his fray-bottomed jeans, it appeared that Binyamin had a seatmate to be reckoned with.

"I'll just squeeze through here," said Binyamin, seeing that his neighbor for the next seven-hour leg of the plane trip had made all the moves he was going to for now.

He shuffled through the cramped space between knees and

the seat in front of them and sat down in his seat with an inward sigh of relief. A pleasant faced, grandmotherly woman beamed congenially at him from her window seat to his left.

"First time traveling?" she asked pleasantly after take-off.

"No," said Binyamin in surprise, as he met the bright blue eyes of his neighbor in the print blouse, seersucker skirt and sensible granny shoes. "Why would you think that?"

Binyamin had only to follow his other neighbor's eyes to realize that his nervous foot tapping was annoying both his neighbors.

"What's up, man?" asked his blond neighbor.

Binyamin instantly stilled the fingers that had been drumming a nervous cadence across the laptop case on his lap. He thought better of putting it under the seat with the hoodlum-like character sitting beside him.

"I'm off to visit the grandchildren," the woman volunteered.

"In Asia?" Binyamin asked in surprise.

"Yes, their father was transferred there just last year," the woman said matter-of-factly. She then reached into her large cloth bag for a well-worn leather photo album. "See, I brought all their pictures along. Aren't they adorable? This is the baby," she said, pointing to a baby in a bassinet. "She just turned two. This is the big boy, John Edward Jr., a chip off the old block. And this is Jessica Beth. Isn't she just an angel? Look at those Shirley Temple curls and that adorable smile. Now here the three of them are in the garden. Can't you just eat them up? Those are the flowers that grew from seeds that I sent them. Can you imagine, my flowers blossoming so far away?"

Binyamin smiled stiffly at the proud grandmother as she stopped for a split second to catch her breath. He had counted on getting some work done on the flight.

After the plane had taken off and drinks and snacks had been served by the stewardess, Binyamin pulled his laptop out of its bag.

"Like a ball and chain, those computer thingamajiggys," muttered the woman as she continued to shuffle through her pictures.

Binyamin powered up his laptop, feeling steel grey eyes shifting attention to him on his right, while the bright blue eyes of the grandmother watched him with equally keen curiosity from over the photos she had suddenly lost interest in as soon as the startup chime of the computer sounded. Binyamin tried to ignore his audience, but he soon realized he was in no frame of mind to look over anything too serious, especially with the unwelcome attention on either side. He decided to relax with a game of solitaire, just to get his mind off of how tense he really felt right now.

Binyamin was well into his second game and finally feeling somewhat calm when he felt a tap on his left arm.

"I'm so sorry for disturbing," said the woman on his left, "but I just had to know. How do you make those cards jump around on the computer screen like that? I know computers have come a long way, but mind reading now, that is really too amazing."

Binyamin demonstrated the laptop's mouse for his enthralled neighbor, and even gave her a try at maneuvering.

"What will they think of next," she said in admiration. Though her moves with the mouse were more than a little shaky, it had been enough to impress her considerably. "My grandchildren have been after me for years now to get a computer, but I tell them that I'm not ready to break down and join the computer generation quite yet. I don't carry a beeper either, or a cell phone, nor do I have an answering machine or call waiting, not even a microwave. 'Old fashioned,' they call me, but I just like to live my life without interference from any machines."

"I can understand that," said Binyamin. "They certainly do complicate life!"

"I can see that," said the older woman sarcastically, as she nodded towards Binyamin's laptop computer, the cell phone clipped onto his pants and the electronic organizer resting on the tray table in front of him.

"Some of us have to live in the here and now," said Binyamin shrugging. "It's how I make my living."

"You don't have to explain any of that to me. Just tell me one thing. If your living makes you so nervous, is it worth it?"

"Worth it?" Binyamin asked in surprise.

"Yes," she said. "You're a nervous wreck. Since the moment you sat down you haven't been able to sit still."

Instantly, Binyamin stopped his foot tapping that had begun again unbeknownst to him.

"All those gadgets and gizmos. ... Maybe a little peace and quiet would be just what the doctor ordered."

"I'm not nervous about business," Binyamin protested.

"Oh," said the woman peering over the top of her bifocals. "You could have fooled me."

"No, really," said Binyamin. "I'm just nervous about my kids."

"Ahh," she said. "And who isn't these days, especially when so many turn out just like him."

She nodded toward Binyamin's right. Binyamin was almost afraid to look, but, much to his relief, he noted out of the corner of his eye that his seatmate on the right was sound asleep, his mouth hanging open. A few strands of hair that had come loose from his ponytail fluttered up and down with each breath he took.

"My kids are much younger," he hastened to explain.

"Little children, little problems, big children, big problems," his seatmate waxed philosophical.

"Actually, it's not really that there's any problem," Binyamin was protesting again.

"Really," she said, looking at the fingers Binyamin was drumming nervously on the armrest between them.

"No, I just hate to leave them when I go on a trip. It's always so hard on them."

"I'm sure their mother will make it up to them," she said with assurance.

"Not this time," said Binyamin. "I'm afraid their mother passed away four years ago."

"I'm *so* sorry," she said and she bit her lip. "The poor poor dears. No wonder you worry! So who's minding the nest—an auntie, granny, good neighbor?"

"A babysitter," said Binyamin. "They've never met her before. That's why I'm a little nervous."

"Never met her!" she exclaimed. "No wonder you're nervous. But you do know this sitter well? She's good with little chicks?"

"I've never actually seen her alone with kids," said Binyamin, clearing his throat nervously, "but she's an amazing person. I'm sure things will be fine."

"Makes one of us," huffed the older woman, looking at Binyamin strangely and then withdrawing into herself and refusing to say another word to him for the remainder of the flight.

Not that Binyamin minded. He was actually rather relieved to be left alone with his own thoughts, though he also felt a little insulted. So what if he had left his kids with a babysitter that they had never met before! Was it really so bad? He ruminated over this during the next several hours. This was the first time he had ever left his kids with a babysitter they had never met before. He had explained it all to them, though, telling them how this trip had come up suddenly, and how he hadn't had much of a choice.

It was too bad that he hadn't had the chance to introduce Shira to them previously. After all, she had worked for him for six months now, and he probably could have found an opportunity to do so. He should've prepared the children better. They liked to make their own decisions about such things. Then again, they were *never* happy when he left them during his extended business trips abroad. Not that he blamed them. It was hard for the three of them to have lost their mother four years ago and to have a father whose jewelry business forced him to travel abroad two or three times year.

Binyamin was certain that Shira was the perfect person to be with his kids right now. He just hoped the children were mature enough to see that as clearly as he did.

SIX

"Lunchtime!" Shira called, her continually cheerful tone already grating on the ears of the two eldest Eisenbergs.

"I wonder what she'll do if we just don't show," said Simcha from the window seat on the landing between the first and second floors.

"I bet she won't even care," said Menucha.

"Less dishes to wash and more food for her to eat herself," said Simcha.

"She isn't *that* fat," said Menucha.

"She isn't fat at all," said Yocheved, glaring at them.

"Kids," Shira called again. "Please come and get it while it's hot."

"Oh, brother," said Simcha, rolling his eyes.

"I'm hungry," said Yocheved, looking from one of her siblings to the other. Not wanting to appear disloyal and suffer the inevitable consequences later, Yocheved hoped one of them at least would change their mind and head down the stairs. "Baila Chana is also hungry."

"Are you guys coming," asked Shira, appearing at the foot of the steps, "or don't you believe in lunch in this house?"

"We're not hungry," muttered Simcha, not even turning to address Shira from his position in the window seat.

"Suit yourselves," said Shira. "I ordered pizza from Zalman's Pizzeria, but if you guys aren't hungry, I'll have to manage what I can on my own."

"Zalman's Pizza!" said Simcha, taking a tentative step towards the stairs.

"With onion rings and garlic-battered cheese sticks," Shira said, nodding pleasantly at the threesome above her.

"Onion rings and garlic-battered cheese sticks," Simcha practically moaned as he pounded down the stairs followed by Yocheved. "I'm coming."

"How did she know the way to Simcha's heart is through his stomach?" Menucha muttered suspiciously as she gazed out the window. "Not to mention that being nice to Baila Chana gets Yocheved every time. Either Tatti really prepared this sitter, or she's just one smart lady."

Creeping into the kitchen later after everyone else had eaten, Menucha opened the pizza box that was still on the table. Six cold, dry and terribly unsavory dried crusts were all that remained of what must have been a wondrous repast. There was no sign of the garlic-battered cheese sticks or any onion rings. Only the greasy cardboard containers that they came in remained. They were scattered across the oak and tile table top and occupied by a scattering of black carpenter ants.

"Looking for something?" Shira asked as Menucha spun around in surprise.

"What are you doing, spying on me?" Menucha asked, her bitter disappointment bubbling forth. "I was just looking at this mess you guys left. My father never lets us leave the room unless the table is first cleared, especially in the summer, since there's such a problem with ants around here. I think we had better call the exterminator again. He came last month, but there are already ants back in the kitchen."

"A few carpenter ants never hurt anyone," said Shira. "I don't like exterminators. Who knows how healthy the stuff they use to kill ants is for the rest of us."

"Tatti *always* calls the exterminator," Menucha insisted stubbornly. "You'll see. The ants just get worse and worse if you don't do something immediately, especially once you leave food out."

"Well, since your father isn't here right now," said Shira, her tone suddenly gentle, "I'll hold off on calling an exterminator right now. So, do you want to come in the other room with us? We're just starting a game of Monopoly. I saved you some food. It's on the counter there all ready to be popped into the microwave."

Menucha just stood there gaping. Shira had actually saved her some cheese sticks and onion rings! Shira had done it again. And had her father told her that Monopoly was her one major weakness, something she could never resist—well, almost never resist?

"I'll pass," Menucha said disdainfully. She wasn't about to fall under Shira's spell as quickly as her siblings had. She was more mature, more sophisticated. But she was also hungry and feeling left out. "Well, maybe I'll just come and watch," she said, feeling the power that Shira's green eyes seemed to exude.

An hour later, though Menucha wasn't sure how, she was knee deep in hotels and properties, having all but wiped the board of all her opponents, Shira included.

"How about some popcorn, and the newest Donny CD?" Shira suggested brightly as Menucha began to clean up the board.

"Tatti didn't let us buy Donny's newest CD," Yocheved said mournfully. "We love all of Donny's tapes, but Tatti made us wait this time."

"Wait no longer," said Shira, reaching into her pocketbook, which she had deposited on the coffee table upon arrival. She pulled out the Donny CD and handed it to an eager Yocheved.

"Wow!" said Simcha. "We've been asking Tatti to buy us this for weeks."

"It's all yours," said Shira.

"See," said Yocheved. "She did bring us a present, and she's not even related!"

"Right," said Shira, unsure of what the seven-year-old really meant, but ready to take any praise that was offered. "Now,

Simcha can put it on, and I'll go pop some popcorn. Come, Yocheved. You show me where the popcorn is."

Menucha watched her two enamored siblings through narrowed eyes. Shira was too smooth. Something was up, she was sure of it. She could almost feel it, but it was too elusive. She just couldn't put her finger on it, but there was plenty of time. Menucha was going to get to the bottom of things. Shira was too cheery, too bright and knew too much, too fast. Pizza, onion rings and garlic-battered cheese sticks? Popcorn and Donny CDs? Shira seemed to have done her homework awfully well—but why?

SEVEN

Monday morning, July 5

"Hello," Shira answered the phone just as Yocheved, the last of the kids to leave for camp, was picked up by bus half an hour late. At least it had shown up before Shira had been forced to drive her herself.

Shira waved a cheerful goodbye at Yocheved through the screen door, thinking all the while how three kids going to three different camps made these kids harder to manage than she felt was necessary, but she quickly lost this train of thought as her caller began to speak.

"Binyamin Eisenberg, please," the crisp, no-nonsense tone rang out sharply, causing Shira to fumble for the volume switch to protect her eardrums.

"He's not home right now," said Shira as she absently stepped on a carpenter ant hurrying across the floor. These ants really were getting to be a nuisance. "Who may I say is calling?"

"This is Mrs. Abromsky," said the overbearing voice. "I must talk to him immediately. To whom am I speaking?"

"This is the sitter," said Shira, spying another ant before she had even cleaned up the remains of the first. "Can I leave him a message?"

"Sitter?" said Mrs. Abromsky. "What does he need a sitter for? All of the children should be off to camp by now. He did tell me that his youngest was seven. Now, if there's someone younger in the picture, then I certainly need to know."

"And why is it that you need to know?" asked Shira, ants forgotten, her eyes narrowing as she verbally fenced with this invisible adversary.

"That's really none of your business, young lady, now is it?"

"I think it really is my business," said Shira. "If you plan on having a message delivered to Mr. Eisenberg, I suggest you provide a few more details before ragging me for personal and private information, like the ages of his children."

"Just like that boy to hire someone so impertinent," the voice huffed.

"He's not quite a boy," said Shira, "and as for impertinent—"

She let her last word hang, her message coming across quite clearly.

"You're right," the caller's tone turned to cloying honey. "He's not a boy. It's just what I'm used to calling all my clients, boys, girls—all presently single. Nasty habit, I agree. Now, what did you say your name was, deary? Maybe you're in the market for a shidduch, too?"

So that was it. Mrs. Abromsky was a shadchan with the delicate mannerisms of a bulldozer. Shira gritted her teeth, even more determined now to get this woman off the phone.

"Oops," she said, as she purposely bumped into the child-size rocker in the playroom where she had wandered with the cordless phone. Baila Chana fell out of the rocker and face-down onto the floor. "Oh no, the baby just took a fall. I have to go!"

"Baby!" spluttered the shadchan indignantly. "Why, this changes everything! He told me the youngest was only se—"

Shira hung up with a satisfying click. She had never been too good at delivering messages. Besides, given the source, she was sure that this was one message Mr. Eisenberg would have no interest in at all.

EIGHT

"I can't believe I forgot my lunch!" Menucha muttered to herself as she turned up the sidewalk towards home. "Really, it's not my fault. Shira saw me leave. She could have reminded me. Isn't that why she's here—to *babysit* us?"

Menucha knew she was being unreasonable, but the heat that was coming off of the sidewalk in waves made it hard to really think straight. It had been hot like this since early morning when she had left for the backyard camp where she worked as a counselor. The job was perfect for her. It gave her a chance to mother all the children that were in her bunk to her heart's content.

Menucha paused right before stepping onto the front porch. She had also forgotten to bring her house key. The car wasn't in the driveway, so Shira was probably out doing the grocery shopping she had mentioned that morning. This wasn't too big of a problem. Menucha went around to the back where the key to the house was hanging in the bike shed, which could be opened only if you knew the combination to the padlock on the door.

A flash of movement caught Menucha's eye as she passed the open window to her father's office, which was off of the kitchen on the ground floor. Menucha had been wrong, dead wrong. Shira was home after all. She must have gone out earlier and then parked the car in the garage, something that the Eisenbergs rarely bothered to do. With her back to the window, Shira stood stooped over the bottom drawer of Mr. Eisenberg's filing cabinet. This drawer was kept locked at all times since it contained, among other things, potential designs for future jewelry pieces along with other confidential information that Mr. Eisenberg felt it wasn't safe to leave out in the open, even at home.

How could Shira have opened the locked drawer? And *why* had Shira opened the locked drawer?

Menucha stood frozen in place. Her heart was thumping loudly in her chest and her mouth seemed suddenly dry. She couldn't believe what she was witnessing!

Concealed by the flowering rhododendron bush, she watched in stunned amazement as Shira withdrew a handful of papers from a file and went over to the fax machine, punching in a number and sending them through the machine one by one. Menucha was too far away to see the number that Shira had entered, but she didn't need to know the number to know one thing for certain. Shira was a spy!

Her father had continually complained about his problems with competitors, including stolen designs, stolen sales tactics, the works. But Menucha had never imagined that her father's competitors would go so far as to place a spy right in the very midst of her family, a spy who had broken into the file that contained the secret innermost workings of her father's business! This was an emergency—big time.

The hidden key forgotten, Menucha turned tail and ran back to camp. The problem of her forgotten lunch was now completely overtaken by the larger danger to her father and to her sister and brother.

NINE

"You got the fax?" Shira asked as she sat in Mr. Eisenberg's home office, behind the large L-shaped, cherry wood desk, tapping nervously on the glass top that had, among other things tucked beneath the surface, a recent, professionally-taken photograph of the Eisenberg family. The warmth of the smiles on their faces caused Shira a momentary pang, but she quickly pushed it away and concentrated on the business at hand.

"It came through just fine," the voice at the other end of the line reported. "Any problems finding the files or getting the filing cabinet open?"

"No," said Shira, "all the files but one were just where you said they would be."

"Now I just need you to find the sketches for the new water pearl collection. I know they're there somewhere. They're in a leather zipper file, not in one of those hanging folders."

"I looked everywhere, even in all the hanging files," said Shira doubtfully. "I checked around the whole room, too. Are you sure it's there?"

"Positive," said the voice. "I must have the plans for the whole new line sent to me if we're going to complete this business successfully! It's the only way we'll be able to go on with our bigger plan!"

"Bigger and *better*," stressed Shira.

"I sure hope so," the tone softened. "But first the water pearl designs."

"I know," sighed Shira. "I'll look again. Maybe they got misfiled, or maybe they're in one of the other drawers, but I don't know how I could miss a file that looks like that. I do wish this was all over already."

"It's necessary," said the voice soothingly. "You know that."

"I can see how important my time here is going to be," said Shira. "I just wish there was some other way, some—"

"We've gone over that already," the voice responded mildly. "You know there's no other way. If there were, we would have done it. This is the only way things can work."

"I understand," said Shira.

"How's it going with the kids?" the voice asked, changing the subject.

"They don't suspect a thing," said Shira, smiling at how easy it had been. "Menucha is a little hard to get through to, but give me some time and I'll have even her eating out of my hand."

"You know what you're there for," said the voice. "I have every faith in you."

"Thank you," said Shira. "I know I'll pull this off—sooner than you think."

"I can't wait," the voice said as Shira smiled to herself, glowing with the pleasure she always felt when speaking to her boss.

"I'll fax you the rest of the diagrams when I find them," she said.

"Perfect."

Still smiling, Shira hung up the phone and turned to continue her search for the recently designed water pearl sketches. She knew it was crucial that she find the designs and fax the copies. Checking her watch to make sure she still had time, she began once again to sift through, under and around each file in the bottom drawer. It had to be here somewhere. If her boss was certain, then so was she.

TEN

"I'm telling you she's a spy," hissed Menucha, walking alongside Simcha.

She had waited forty-five minutes in the hot sun until he got home from camp, not daring to brave the interior of the house on her own with Shira there.

"Now you're really getting carried away," said Simcha. "I know you don't like her because she's here doing all the work that you think you can do yourself. But come on, Menucha, a spy? Give me a break!"

"So don't believe me," said Menucha, "but I'm going to get proof."

"Oh yeah?" said a skeptical Simcha. "How?"

"I'll think of something," said Menucha.

"I'm sure you will," said Simcha, rolling his eyes.

"Let's go get Yocheved," said Menucha. "She went to play at Aviva's house after camp. I'm supposed to pick her up at five."

"I'll just go in the house and get a drink," said Simcha.

"Don't go in by yourself!" Menucha panicked. "Who knows what she'll do to you. Just open the front door, drop off your camp bag, holler to her that you're going out to play now and close the door before she has a chance to reply! That's what I did."

"You really are serious about this, aren't you?" Even though Simcha was skeptical, Menucha was more often right than wrong.

"Of course I am serious," said Menucha. "I'm telling you, she's a spy."

"If she's after the files from Tatti's office," said Simcha thinking out loud, "because she's working for Tatti's competition, then let's do this…"

Simcha leaned over to whisper to his sister, as if the bushes might be eavesdropping. Menucha nodded in appreciation. Simcha had an amazing idea. The trap would be set tomorrow.

ELEVEN

"Hello?"

"Hello," said an unmistakable shrill feminine voice.

Shira fumbled for the volume control, dropping it several notches for instant relief.

"This is Mrs. Abromsky."

"I know," Shira said, leaning against the nearest wall for support. "But I told you yesterday that Mr. Eisenberg is out of town."

"So I heard," said the caller. "I heard more, too."

"I beg your pardon," said Shira nervously.

"How about you explain to me the little game you are playing."

"What game?" asked Shira. "I really don't have time for games. I have enough to do just looking after the children."

"And the baby?" Mrs. Abromsky prodded.

"The baby?" said Shira in puzzlement. "Oh right, the baby."

"There is no baby," Mrs. Abromsky snapped.

"Sure there is," Shira argued weakly. "She just turned seven. She's still the baby, though."

"I need to speak to Mr. Eisenberg," said Mrs. Abromsky. "I have a shidduch for him, a nice girl, nice home, nice manners."

Everything you're not, the woman's tone seemed to imply to Shira.

"A *bas tz'nuah, baalas midos, derech eretz*, a gem, *mamish* a gem."

"Why are you telling me all this?" asked Shira flatly.

"So you'll give him the message."

"He's out of town right now. It won't do him much good to get your message."

"That's for him to decide, wouldn't you say?" asked the shadchan. "And once you've delivered your message, give me a call and we'll talk. Maybe I have just the right boy for you." And with that the phone went dead.

TWELVE

"I still don't understand how you can be so sure she'll have noticed it," Menucha was saying as she strode along beside her brother.

"Elementary, my dear Watson," Simcha said as he hurried up the front path, eager to find out if his trap had been sprung. "I told her that I had found one of Tatti's files on the bookshelf in the living room so just in case Tatti called she could tell him. I even mentioned that it was probably one of his really important files, but I couldn't be sure."

"Didn't she ask to see it?" Menucha asked.

"Sure," said Simcha. "I told her that if it was top secret I wasn't allowed to show it to her. Then I told her that I was going to hide the file in my room until I speak to Tatti so he could tell me what to do with it."

"What's the file really?" Menucha asked.

"It's nothing," said Simcha. "It's just an old file with some out-of-date jewelry catalogues he gave me once for school when we had to do a report on what our fathers worked at, but she doesn't know that. If she's a spy, I bet she'll search my room for it. If she searches the room, we'll find out. If she's not a spy, she won't bother going in my room, and we'll know that, too."

"We're home!" Simcha called as the pair entered the front hall.

"Hi guys," Shira called.

"Hi, Simcha and Menucha," Yocheved echoed from the kitchen. "Guess what Shira made! Chocolate chip brownies! Come and have some. The chips are all melty. She's going to show me how to make them tomorrow."

"Later," Simcha called as he and Menucha thundered up the stairs.

"Okay," Simcha said, pausing outside his bedroom door. "The first trap has been sprung."

They both bent to examine the door knob. As Simcha said, the light coating of baking powder that he had sprinkled across the top of the door knob had been wiped nearly clean from a hand turning the knob.

"Maybe she just came in to check if your bed is made or something," said Menucha.

"Maybe," said Simcha. "Let's go find out."

Simcha thrust the door to his bedroom open and marched across the room to check his desk drawers. Menucha followed at a slower pace, carefully picking her way across the clothing, shoes, books and other assorted debris that were strewn across her brother's floor and across every available surface. Simcha was not known for keeping his room particularly neat.

"Bingo!" he declared enthusiastically from beside his desk. "Every drawer has been opened."

"The dresser, too," said Menucha as she examined each drawer.

It was easy to tell, since every drawer had had one of Yocheved's long hairs taken from her hairbrush and planted so that it was sticking out of the middle of each drawer to hang over the side. They had done it earlier that morning. Simcha had checked right before leaving for camp, and every single hair had been in place. Now, though, every drawer was missing its hair, which could only have happened if the drawers had been opened that day.

"She's a spy all right," said Simcha in wonder. "You're right, Menucha. She even opened the file. See?"

Menucha leaned over to look at the file Simcha had buried in his bottom drawer. Simcha had lined up the three color catalogues he had put inside the manila folder so that each was slightly misaligned but with precision, exactly one-fourth of an inch each. Now though, they were neatly lined up inside the folder.

"So now what do we do?" Menucha asked, suddenly feeling overwhelmed.

"We have to tell Tatti," said Simcha, shrugging. "What else?"

"Fine," said Menucha, "let's call his cell phone now."

"Great idea," said Simcha, reaching for the extension on his desk. "I'll call. I just hope he's not in the middle of some important meeting or something."

"If he is," said Menucha, "he'll have the phone on vibrate, and he'll just call us back when he can speak."

Simcha dialed with Menucha looking over his shoulder, and leaning in close to hear her father when he answered.

"It's ringing," said Simcha unnecessarily.

"I can hear that," said Menucha.

"One ring," Simcha counted out loud, much to Menucha's irritation, "two rings, three rings."

"Hello," a startlingly familiar voice said.

"Yocheved?" Simcha said. "What are you doing there? I thought you were downstairs."

"I was," Yocheved said reasonably, "but the phone was ringing, so I got it."

"The phone wasn't ringing," said Simcha. "I was on it."

"I know you're on it," Yocheved said. "Why are you calling?"

"Oh, give me that phone," said Menucha, taking the phone from her brother and putting it to her own ear. "Yocheved, are you still in the kitchen?"

"Menucha," said Yocheved accusingly. "You also left and didn't tell me? Maybe I wanted to come."

"I didn't leave," said Menucha. "I'm right here. Where are you?"

"I'm right here," answered Yocheved simply.

"Right where?" said Menucha. "I can't see you when you're on the phone. Where are you?"

"Here. Right here," said Yocheved again, as Menucha shook off Simcha's arm. Was he trying to get the phone back?

"Over there," Simcha hissed when his sister brushed him off yet again.

Menucha turned towards Simcha, and towards the doorway where Yocheved stood.

"Where did you get that cell phone?" asked Menucha.

"It was ringing on Tatti's desk in his office," Yocheved still spoke into the phone. "So I answered it."

"Yocheved," said Menucha before realizing how silly she must look talking into the phone with her sister only a few feet away. "Here. Give me that. Why did Tatti leave his cell phone?"

She hung up both phones, staring at her father's cell phone in her hands with consternation.

"There you kids are," said Shira brightly as she appeared in the doorway. "Why don't you help yourselves to the fresh brownies downstairs in the kitchen? Don't worry, Simcha, I made them without nuts so you can have them."

"Thanks, Shira," said Simcha with a grin.

"Afterwards we can go outside," said Shira. "It's such a beautiful day. How about a game of croquet, or we can go for a walk to the park or—"

"Yeah! Let's go to the park!" said Yocheved.

"I wouldn't mind—" Simcha said as well.

"No thank you," interrupted Menucha coldly as her siblings gave her hurt looks. "We'll pass."

"What's Tatti's cell phone doing here?" Yocheved asked, ignoring the glare that her sister gave her.

"Oh, that," said Shira. "He left it here for me to use."

"He left *you* his cell phone?" said Menucha incredulously.

"Sure," said Shira, "to take with me whenever we go out, and to have in case you kids need anything. He wanted to make sure I would only be seconds from the phone."

"But what about him?" asked Simcha.

"He bought another one for himself," said Shira. "He decided to get a satellite cell phone to make sure it would work wherever he was traveling."

"What's the number?" asked Simcha bluntly.

"I'm not sure," said Shira with a shrug. "I wrote it down somewhere when he gave it to me. Why? Do you guys want to talk to him about something?"

"No," said Menucha, instantly on guard. "We were just curious."

"Okay," said Shira. "There's still chocolate chip brownies downstairs if you want them."

The threesome followed Shira out the door, Menucha hesitating for only a fraction of a second before coming to the conclusion that brownies, even baked by a spy, were still brownies.

THIRTEEN

Tuesday afternoon, July 6

"It's your favorite neighborhood crank," the voice cackled over Officer Scott's walkie-talkie.

"Oh no, not her again," Officer Scott groaned. "What is it this time?"

"Someone has stolen her tulips or something like that."

"Give me a break," said Officer Scott.

"She's reporting a robbery," the voice squawked mercilessly. "You're the nearest officer. I suggest you respond."

"Why me? Why me?" Officer Scott muttered to himself over and over as he turned his car and headed towards 1442 Sobey Road.

It was at times like this that he really wondered why he had left the big city to work in a dinky little town like New

Hempstead. Nothing ever happened here like things had in the city. If nothing ever happened, there was no chance to excel, no chance for promotion and no chance to go anywhere but out the door at age 65, still the same placid, tame, bored and boring police officer who had taken the job when he was young and fiery and full of promise at age twenty-five.

Officer Scott pulled into the driveway no more cheerful than when he had started towards his destination. He got out of the car and went up to the door, which was flung open before he had even reached the porch.

"Took you long enough," Mrs. Rosenman glared at him.

"Good morning, Ma'am," Officer Scott said, trying to be friendly.

"Maybe for you it is, but it hasn't been for me once I saw that my beautiful purple hostas had been stolen, cut down in their prime. What's a body to do? I can't watch everything every minute now, can I?"

"I guess not, Ma'am," said Officer Scott, trying to keep his tone of voice polite and patient. "How about you lead me to the scene of this alleged crime?"

"*Alleged*," Mrs. Rosenman sniffed, shuffling down the walk and stepping into the grass and over to a well-kept rock garden. "They're gone, aren't they? Every single stalk of flowers from my hostas has disappeared, and I didn't give anyone permission now, did I? That's what I call stolen, nothing *alleged* about that."

"Could be," said Officer Scott noncommittally as he knelt to study the dirt beside the patch of long, fat leaves with white stripes down the middle, now prematurely bereft of their purple blooms, though a straggly end here and there still stuck out from amidst the thick leaves. "Looks like a deer track to me."

"Those neighborhood children," Mrs. Rosenman was saying, "are always scampering through my yard. One day I caught a little boy decapitating my marigolds, and another day it was a little girl after my pansies. I'm telling you, nothing is safe in this world anymore. Can't trust the neighborhood kids, can't trust the hired help." Here she looked darkly across the street at the Eisenbergs' house. "What's safe anymore, if flowers disappear from under your own nose in your own yard?"

"Now that's a good question, Ma'am," said Officer Scott, straightening and brushing the dirt off of his hands. "But it seems pretty cut and dry to me that—"

He stopped as his radio squawked again.

"Suspect with a gun reported wearing blue jeans, yellow T-shirt and a gorilla mask heading north down Main Street."

"I'm really sorry, Ma'am," Officer Scott said as he turned up the volume of his walkie-talkie and tried to calm his heart that was now pumping a mile a minute with sudden energy—a real crime for a change! "But I think we're going to have to cut this short."

"You can't do that!" Mrs. Rosenman gasped. "You haven't even looked for clues or taken a full report."

"I'm sorry, Mrs. Rosenman," Officer Scott said as he reached into the back seat of his jeep, "but I have to be going. If I were you I would just keep an eye on the deer and not on the neighbor's kids. I think that's your best bet, if you want my advice."

"Advice! If I wanted advice I wouldn't have called a police officer."

"Next time do me the favor," Officer Scott muttered under his breath as he opened the back seat of his jeep.

"What's that for?" Mrs. Rosenman asked as he pulled out a seldom used, slate grey, padded vest and pulled it on over his drab, grey uniform.

"Don't want to spring a leak now, do I?" he said, straightening the bulletproof vest before climbing into his car. "Best of luck. I do hope your flowers recover."

"Not a chance of that," she said, shaking her head in disgust as he pulled away. "They only bloom once a year and now the blooms are all gone, as if you cared."

FOURTEEN

Tuesday afternoon, July 6

"Why do you want to call Tatti?" asked Yocheved around a mouthful of chocolate chip brownie as the three sat around the white formica kitchen table, enjoying the after-camp snack that Shira had baked for them.

"Who says we do?" asked Simcha reaching for a brownie.

"Well, you were calling him before," said Yocheved logically.

"Who says?" said Simcha.

"Well, if you weren't calling him," said Yocheved, "then how come his phone rang?"

"Maybe we dialed wrong," said Menucha.

"Then who were you trying to call?" asked Yocheved.

"Maybe the doctor," said Menucha, reaching out a hand to

stop Yocheved from helping herself to another brownie, as the chocolate smeared on her face and the crumbs on the table attested that it was obviously nowhere near her first or second piece. "Since you're going to have a major stomachache if you eat any more of those chocolate chip brownies."

"Am not," sulked Yocheved, reaching with her other hand past Menucha and cramming a large mouthful in. "Shira said I could eat all I want."

"Well, Shira is not your mother," said Menucha.

"And neither are you," said Yocheved around a thick, gooey mouthful.

"No more brownies, Yocheved," Menucha said, pushing the plate towards Simcha so that he won the grab for the biggest chocolate chip brownie.

"I was just getting one for you," said Yocheved sweetly.

"I bet you were," said Menucha, "and even if you were, do you think I would have wanted you to touch it with your hands like that?"

"No," said Yocheved brightly, "that way, I would have had to eat it for you."

"You're all heart," said Menucha, reaching over for a tissue to attend to the three ants by her feet. It seemed that chocolate brownies had a way of calling to ants as well as to children. "I really think we should call an exterminator already."

"Oh, that again," said Shira as she came into the kitchen, her arms loaded with food supplies from the garage. She glanced over as Menucha picked up the ants and threw them into the garbage. "No wonder you have a problem. What do you think, that they just stay in the garbage because you put them there?"

"You have to squish them," said Simcha.

"I don't like feeling them when I squeeze," said Menucha with a shudder.

"I just take them outside," said Yocheved.

"That's better than throwing them whole into the garbage," said Shira. "If you do that, they just march right back out into the kitchen, just like those three are climbing out of the garbage now."

"I don't want to kill ants," said Menucha. "That's why Tatti gets an exterminator."

"So someone else can do your dirty work," said Simcha, as he walked over and squashed the ants one by one.

"I don't want to talk about this anymore," said Menucha.

"Does that mean you don't want brownies anymore either?" asked Simcha.

"Not right now," said Menucha. "I just think we should call the exter—"

"Well, we aren't going to," Shira interrupted. "I already told you that I don't like taking a chance with those chemicals around children, and I don't think a few ants here and there are a real problem."

"Fine," said Menucha, "just don't expect me to squish them if I see any."

"Just call me in," said Simcha. "I'll take care of them for you."

"And for me," said Yocheved, sliding her thumb into her mouth while nervously twisting a strand of hair, uncomfortable with the notion of squished ants.

"I'll take care of them for you, too," Simcha answered. "But please get your thumb out of your mouth! What are you, a baby?"

"I was just getting the brownie crumbs off," protested Yocheved, embarrassed at her brother having caught her in the act.

"I'm just going to start a lasagna for supper," said Shira. "You guys like lasagna, don't you?"

"Just so long as it's not too *spy*-cy," said Simcha, drawing out the word.

There was no reaction from Shira, though Menucha elbowed him sharply in the side.

"Watch it," she hissed in Simcha's ear, but he only laughed as he made a grab for his second brownie.

"So what now?" Menucha whispered to Simcha as Shira disappeared into the pantry in search of some ingredient.

"Beats me," said Simcha with a shrug. "I guess we wait for Tatti to call here."

"What good—" Menucha began before she was brought up short by Shira's reentry with a jar of marinara sauce.

"The chocolate chip brownies *are* good, aren't they?" Shira beamed at Menucha, who only glared at Shira's back as she cut and chopped up an onion to add to the tomato sauce. "I was going to wait to bake them with you kids, but I realized you would be too hungry when you got home from camp to wait, so I did them on my own. Maybe after supper we can all bake something else together for tomorrow unless you want to play another game of Monopoly or—"

"I want to bake hamantashen," interrupted Yocheved.

"Hamantashen?" said Shira, turning puzzled.

"Yeah, hamantashen," Yocheved insisted. "Menucha wouldn't let me this year, and it was no fair."

"We got enough hamantashen in the *shalach manos*," Menucha explained. "You never eat them anyway. You just like to bake them, and then I'm stuck taking baggies of hamantashen for snacks to school after they've been left in the freezer for who knows how long."

"I know how long," said Simcha matter-of-factly. "You take them to school until we have to clean out the freezer for Pesach."

"I want chocolate ones, too," Yocheved insisted. "Menucha never lets me make chocolate hamantashen."

"You never asked," said Menucha.

"If we make chocolate ones," Yocheved went on, ignoring her sister, "then there wouldn't be any left over. We all love chocolate."

"Okay," said Shira cheerfully. "Chocolate hamantashen it is."

"It's summer time," Menucha insisted.

"There's no *halacha* against baking hamantashen in the summer," said Shira. "I think it sounds like fun."

Yocheved grinned broadly as Menucha shot daggers at Shira's back.

Glancing over towards Yocheved moments later, Menucha noticed tears streaming down her sister's face, leaving streaks in the smears of chocolate that encrusted either cheek.

"What's wrong now, Yocheved?" Menucha asked as she went over to gather her sister onto her lap.

"Yeah," said Simcha, looking up in surprise. "Why are you crying?"

"I'm not crying," said Yocheved, sniffing loudly. "It's just my eyes are running."

"What's the diff—" Menucha began.

"Oh, you poor dear," said Shira, turning to scoop Yocheved into her arms, which wasn't that easy to do as Yocheved was rather tall for her age. "Come, I'll wash off your face and get you away from this nasty smelling onion. See, it has me crying, too?"

Menucha watched in disgust as her sister was carried out of the room like a baby while Yocheved peered over Shira's shoulder with a self-satisfied expression on her face.

"So now what?" asked Menucha, getting down to business right away as soon as Shira was out of earshot.

"I said we wait for Tatti to call," Simcha volunteered.

"And I was going to say how good—" Menucha said.

"—how good the brownies are," said Simcha, repeating Shira's misinterpretation with a laugh.

"No," said Menucha, "I wanted to say how good do you think it will be for us if Shira is in the room when Tatti calls—like she was every minute last night, like he's her father or something? We can't tell him anything if she's going to be there."

"Leave it to me," said Simcha, smiling wisely. "I know just the trick, but you'll have to be the one to tell him, and you'll have to tell him fast because I'm not sure how long I can keep Shira out of the room."

"It's a deal," said Menucha as Simcha reached for the last brownie on the blue and white plate.

"It was really nice of her to remember not to make them with nuts," he mused, pausing with his hand still over the plate.

"Yeah, real nice," said Menucha sarcastically. "Wait! How did she know that you're allergic to nuts?"

"Beats me," said Simcha, the chocolate chip brownie momentarily forgotten. "I didn't tell her."

"Neither did I," Menucha remarked thoughtfully, "and why would Yocheved?"

"So how did she know?" Simcha asked.

"Because she's a spy," said Menucha. "It's just further proof against her."

"If you say so," said Simcha. "I'm just glad she did her research on us so well, or I wouldn't be eating these right now."

"You aren't," said Menucha with a self-satisfied smile.

"What do you mean I'm not?" Simcha asked.

"They're all gone now," said Menucha.

"Hey," yelled Simcha, "you took the last brownie, and it was mine!"

"You already had too many," said Menucha.

"Who are you to judge?" asked Simcha as he lurched out of his seat to make a grab at his sister and the last of his brownie.

Menucha was too fast, though. She was already out of her seat and racing towards the door before Simcha could get her. The last of the chocolate chip brownie disappeared into her mouth as Simcha closed in on her. Just then, the phone rang.

"I'll get it," Simcha called out as Menucha froze in her tracks behind him.

Maybe it was Tatti, and if they got to the phone before Shira—

"Hello," Simcha said, as Menucha came up behind him to listen in as well.

"Shira already got it," he said, hanging up in disgust.

"What does she think?" Menucha asked angrily. "Does she think that this is her house? You said you were getting the phone."

"Maybe she didn't hear me," said Simcha with a shrug.

"Who was it?" Menucha asked

"How should I know?" asked Simcha.

"Pick it up again!" said Menucha, and quietly. "Maybe it's her *connection*."

"Her *connection*?" said Simcha.

"Yeah," said Menucha. "She has to be spying for someone. Maybe she's giving over some information right now."

"It's not nice to listen in on other people's conversations," Simcha stated.

"She's a *spy*," said Menucha. "If she can spy on us, we can spy on her!"

"I don't know," said Simcha, clearly bothered.

"She's here to destroy Tatti's business!" said Menucha. "She may bake good brownies, get us other amazing food, play games with us and bring us presents, but, Simcha, she's a spy. It's her job to make us happy so we won't be suspicious and so she can find out all of Tatti's secrets."

"Oh, all right," said Simcha, pulling the phone slowly off the hook.

He listened for several seconds before replacing the receiver.

"Who was it?" Menucha asked.

"I don't know," said Simcha unhappily. "She already hung up."

FIFTEEN

Wednesday afternoon, July 7

"You want to what?"

Menucha had to hold the phone well away from her ear as Shira's screech had proved dangerous to her eardrums.

"Who's she yelling at?" Simcha mouthed, looking up from the book he was perusing while sitting on a chair with his feet resting on Menucha's bed.

Menucha, glaring pointedly at her brother's shoes on her purple, flowered comforter, held a finger to her lips and pressed her ear closer to the phone again.

"You're not really serious," Shira was saying. "I can't have you here now. It could jeopardize—well, you just *can't* come and that's final!"

"I'll be there in half an hour," the calm voice replied, completely ignoring Shira's tone. "I'm in the neighborhood, and I don't see any reason why I shouldn't."

"But I'm not ready for you!" Shira sounded near panic.

"Ready or not, here I come," the tone sounded teasing.

Menucha waited until she heard two clicks, the stranger's and Shira's, before pressing the off button on the cordless phone.

"Someone's coming," she said almost breathlessly in answer to Simcha's unspoken question.

"Who? When?" Simcha asked, letting out the breath he had been holding in a sudden whoosh.

"I don't know," said Menucha in a panic, "but Shira didn't want the visit. She sounded upset. That's all I know, except that Shira kept saying no and it didn't do much good. Whoever this woman is, she'll be here in half an hour. I'm sure it's her connection. Shira said she wasn't ready, but this woman refused to listen. I bet Shira doesn't have the information they want yet. I bet that's why Shira sounded so nervous. I bet—"

"Whatever," said Simcha. "We have half an hour. We'll watch Shira like a hawk and we'll listen in. That way we'll know for sure!"

But Shira had other plans.

SIXTEEN

"Ko-shur," Binyamin pronounced the word slowly and clearly for the little Chinese man standing behind what seemed to be an ancient register at the counter of the narrow, closet-sized space that he had been directed to when he had asked about a grocery.

He had already searched up and down the dingy, narrow aisles of the little store. He had examined bottles and jars one by one, much to the puzzlement of the store's proprietor who had never seen a Jew shopping for kosher symbols, in a vain attempt at finding something he could eat.

"Ah, ko-shur," the man aped back as understanding seemed to light his features, much to Binyamin's relief. Binyamin straightened up and wiped his hands on his pants after replacing the jar of pickled pig's feet that he had mistaken for something more palatable.

Binyamin had traveled to China previously, but never to this part of China. In the past he had always been able to find additions to the staples that he brought with him without too much trouble. Some unidentified individual on the kosher forum that he had visited online before making this trip had promised him up and down that he would have little trouble finding kosher food in the local stores if he just knew how to look. Binyamin had been doubtful at first, but decided to take his chances and had traveled light this time. Already, though, he was tired of the peanut butter and tuna on matzah that had been his staple diet over the last few days.

"Very good," the proprietor was saying, nodding vigorously. "Yes, have ko-shur."

The little man stepped lithely from behind the counter and disappeared down one of the narrow aisles, returning with a dusty glass jar.

"Pickles?" Binyamin said, once he had wiped some of the dust from the surface of the jar.

"Ko-shur," the man said, pointing to the words beneath some unrecognized brand name, *kosher dill spears*.

"Yes, I see," Binyamin said, hurriedly surveying the jar for a kosher symbol he recognized. Amazingly enough, the pickles really were kosher. "I'll take it," Binyamin said as the little man bobbed and smiled pleasantly.

"Well," said Binyamin to himself as he left the dark and dingy store behind. "I suppose I could call this a vegetable, and I haven't had any of those since I got here so I won't complain. The price is right, too. I didn't do too badly after all."

SEVENTEEN

"Okay," said Menucha.

"Why are you whispering?" asked Simcha.

"I guess I'm just nervous," said Menucha in her regular tone of voice.

"It wasn't too hard finding Tatti's number," said Simcha. "He hung his whole list on the refrigerator where he always leaves it."

"Yeah," said Menucha. "So, I didn't think of that. It happens. I was just all upset that he got a new phone since the only thing I could think about was that I only knew the number to the old one."

"Yeah," said Simcha. "So are you going to dial?"

"Should I call his cell phone," asked Menucha, studying the list of numbers her father had left, "or should I call the hotel?"

"Call the cell phone," said Simcha. "At least only Tatti picks up that phone. You never know about the hotel phone. Maybe they can listen in when they forward the calls to the rooms."

"Talk about paranoid," said Menucha as she began punching in numbers. "I just hope he answers. I think it's the middle of the night there, but this is a real emergency. We have to talk to him now."

Simcha leaned in closer. After three rings, he heard his father's recorded voice.

"This is Binyamin Eisenberg. Please leave me a message so I can get back to you. Thanks."

"What do I do?" hissed Menucha, covering up the mouthpiece before the beep.

"Leave him a message," said Simcha with a shrug. "Do you have a choice? You're the one who said it was an emergency."

"Hi, Tatti," said Menucha. "I really need to speak to you. It's important, so call me back as soon as you can. Oh, and don't tell Shira I called. Really—it's a matter of life or death."

"What's that supposed to mean?" asked Simcha as she hung up.

"It's important," said Menucha. "You know that."

"Sure," said Simcha, "but you don't want him all panicky for nothing. After all, no one's dying."

"Not if I can help it," said Menucha grimly.

EIGHTEEN

Binyamin slid his electronic key into the door lock of his hotel room. A scant few hours ago he had gotten up late and rushed out to his first meeting of the day. He'd had barely enough time to *daven*. All he could think about now was how exhausted he felt.

The light on the phone switched to green as the door unlocked. He slipped inside and, automatically, glanced over to the telephone. The light on the phone was not flashing so he had no phone messages, which was a relief. He was always nervous about the kids when he was away. That's why he always carried his cell phone. But after years of experience, he knew that the cell phone wasn't one hundred percent reliable, especially here in a foreign country. He made a mental note to call Shira and the kids that night. With the twelve-hour time difference he should be able to catch them before they left for camp in the morning. Until then, he was just going to take a little nap.

Though jet lag had rarely bothered him much on any of his previous trips, Binyamin failed to realize that this was one trip where he had started off already drained of sleep. So after a couple of days of being awake at all the wrong hours and half asleep during even worse times, he felt especially hard hit. So hard hit, as a matter of fact, that he didn't awaken when the cell phone that was still buried in his jacket pocket started its muffled ringing. Binyamin was dead to the world.

NINETEEN

"Menucha, Simcha, Yocheved!" Shira called from the foot of the stairs. "I need to speak to you guys for a minute."

Menucha and Simcha exchanged glances. After leaving the message for their father, they had spent the next fifteen minutes making plans in Menucha's room to make sure that they didn't miss a single word that went on between Shira and her unwelcome visitor.

Yocheved had been playing in her room. She was already down the stairs before Menucha and Simcha had even left their room.

"Menucha and Simcha!" Shira called again.

"I think she means us," said Simcha, getting up from the desk chair with a sigh.

"I wonder what she wants," Menucha mused.

"There's only one way to find out," said Simcha, as he headed towards the stairs.

"There you are," said Shira as she stood tapping her foot impatiently at the foot of the stairs. "You might not believe this, but all three of you have been invited to visit friends now."

"All three of us?" asked Menucha suspiciously. "By whom?"

"Simcha has been invited by Yehuda," said Shira, ticking off the friends one by one on her fingers. "Yocheved by Yael, and Menucha by Ahuva."

"Why would the Cohnens invite all three of us? Yocheved isn't even Yael's age."

"I know," said Shira, smiling brightly. "Strange isn't it, but I suppose Mrs. Cohnen figured that if she's having a friend over for the other two, she might as well invite Yocheved, too."

"Yocheved doesn't want to play with someone younger than her," said Menucha.

"I don't mind," said Yocheved as she snuggled close to Shira. "Shira's going to take us all out for ice cream later if we go nicely."

"Oh," said Menucha, her eyes narrowing at the lowness of Shira bribing Yocheved with ice cream.

"Ice cream?" said Simcha, exchanging an imploring look with Menucha. The look of fury on her face was more than enough to convince him, though. "I think I'll pa—"

"Ice cream and an afternoon at the Cohnen's sounds just right," Menucha interrupted.

Shira smiled in obvious relief.

"It does?" said Simcha in surprise.

"Yes, it does," said Menucha. "When are we supposed to go over?"

"Real soon," said Shira, checking her watch somewhat nervously.

"Sure thing," said Menucha sweetly. "It was so nice of Mrs. Cohnen to call and invite us over like that—all three of us."

"Yes, it was. Wasn't it?" said Shira somewhat doubtfully.

"Well, if we were invited," said Menucha, "I guess we'd better leave already. We don't want to keep them waiting. Funny, though, I don't remember hearing the phone ring."

"You do have call waiting," said Shira, blushing furiously. "And I was on the other line before."

Shira hadn't exactly lied, but it wasn't the truth either. Menucha knew that. She had been listening in when Shira had been on her last call, unless she had called someone else between then, which Menucha thought was highly unlikely given the time constraints.

"So what do we do now?" Simcha asked as the three strode determinedly down the driveway after Shira had shooed them all out the door.

"We're stopping over at the Cohnens to tell them that we can't come," said Menucha.

"Why are we stopping over?" asked Simcha, not particularly caring for the heat and humidity. "How about if we just call?"

"We can't," said Menucha. "Shira's still home."

"But won't Shira still—"

"Stop with all the questions already, Simcha," said Menucha. "Don't worry. I have it all figured out and we have to hurry, too. We don't want to miss Tatti's call."

"There's Mrs. Rosenman," Yocheved interrupted cheerily as she waved vigorously to the face peeking from their next-door neighbor's curtain.

"Stop that, Yocheved." Menucha said.

"Why?" asked a hurt Yocheved.

"She doesn't want you to see her," said Menucha.

"Is that why she always hides behind the curtain?" Yocheved said. "She always does it. When I leave for camp, she's there. When I go to school, she watches. When I play outside, she's always standing there at the window. Why do you think she doesn't want me to wave when I see her?"

"Because she likes to pretend she's not watching," said Menucha. "That's why she hides behind the curtain, and that's why she went away as soon as you waved. She likes to watch, but she doesn't want us to know it."

"Why do you think that is?" Simcha asked, suddenly curious about the woman always peeking at them.

"I think she doesn't have anything else to do," said Menucha shrugging. "So she watches us."

"Weird," said Simcha.

"Sad," said Menucha.

"Yeah, I guess," said Simcha as Yocheved, having lost interest in the conversation, skipped ahead. "Anyway back to the

Cohnens. So I have no problem going to hang out with Yehuda, but I thought you wanted—"

"Shhh," cautioned Menucha, as Yocheved skipped back towards them, jumping over every crack in the sidewalk as she went along.

"Oh, right," said Simcha, getting Menucha's drift not to spill the beans around Yocheved.

Seven minutes later, they turned into the Cohnens' driveway. Yocheved stopped to study the decorated mailbox grounded in a barrel flowerpot of blooming snapdragons. The mailbox had been painted by Yael's oldest sister, Nechama. The images of delicate flowers and an ornate wooden bridge held her entranced as she stepped around to view the mailbox from every angle.

"Can we go now?" Menucha asked impatiently. "You've only seen the mailbox about a million times already."

"I know," said Yocheved, "but I like looking at it. It's so pretty."

Exasperated, Menucha went on ahead to ring the doorbell. Simcha followed.

"The door's open," called a voice from inside.

"Come on in," Mrs. Cohnen looked down at them from the railing in the kitchen that overlooked the entranceway. "The kids are waiting for you downstairs."

"Oh, we can't stay," said Menucha.

"Can't stay?" said Simcha, who was enjoying the coolness inside after the humid heat they had just walked through.

"Something came up again with Shira," said Menucha, picking her words carefully to avoid an outright lie," so she doesn't need us to come after all. We just came by to let you know."

"She doesn't?" Yocheved asked, her eyes widening in surprise.

"You walked over here in this heat just to tell me that?" said Mrs. Cohnen, her brown eyes reflecting her puzzled frown. "Well, I'm glad to hear that whatever Shira's emergency was, it's over."

"What? They're leaving? But they just got here," said Mr. Cohnen, getting up from the white leather living room couch to peer down at the threesome in the front hall, half a flight down. "The kids will be disappointed since Annie already told them that you were coming. Maybe you can visit another time."

"Yes, I know. I'm sorry," said Menucha to Mrs. Cohnen, and then she turned to Yocheved. "We're *not* staying."

"Well, I *am*," said Yocheved vehemently.

"She can stay," said Mrs. Cohnen. "Yael was really looking forward to having her."

"It's all right," said Menucha. "We really have to go home."

"I'm *staying*!" Yocheved insisted again.

"But Shira needs us at home," wheedled Simcha.

"She said we should come here," said Yocheved.

"That was before," said Menucha, her face flushing red as Mrs. Cohnen watched this rather curious scene unfold.

"You made it all up," said Yocheved. "She told me—"

"She told you that before," reasoned Simcha, "but maybe Menucha knows that she changed her mind afterwards."

"Nuh-uh," said Yocheved stubbornly from around the thumb that had crept unnoticed into her mouth. "She promised."

"Ah, so that's it," said Menucha with relief. "Don't worry, you'll still get the ice cream that Shira promised."

"If you get that thumb out of your mouth already," said Simcha. "You look like such a baby."

"I am not a baby!" Yocheved glared.

"That's right you're not," said Menucha. "That's why you're big enough to go out for ice cream."

"We'll buy it for you later," said Simcha. "Though if you want to stay—"

"No, that's okay," said Yocheved, finally yielding. "I'm coming home, too."

"They're here!" Yael called stampeding down the hall to greet Yocheved.

"Hi, Yael! Sorry, we're actually leaving," said Menucha as Ahuva appeared in the hallway above, her dark, tight curls pulled back in a short pony.

"You're not staying?" asked Yael, a miniature reflection of Ahuva right down to the dark curls.

"Maybe we'll come back later," said Simcha, grinning at Yehuda, who had suddenly appeared behind Ahuva. "I can come by later, and we can play basketball."

"Fine," said Yehuda with an easygoing shrug, as Yael stooped down to peer through the railing between Yehuda and Ahuva's legs.

"Thanks for having us," Menucha called politely as the three rushed out and waved goodbye to the Cohnens.

Menucha breathed a sigh of relief. She thought they would never get out of there.

"So now what?" asked Simcha as they headed for home. "And how did you know that Mrs. Cohnen wasn't the one who invited us?"

"Just a hunch," said Menucha. "And as for what now, I don't know. Let's wait and see."

"I wanted to play," said Yocheved grumpily.

"No, you didn't," soothed Menucha. "Yael is way too young for you. You just wanted ice cream."

"Okay," said Yocheved. "I want ice cream."

"We'll get you ice cream later," said Menucha. "Just behave yourself, and do what I say for a little while longer. Then I'll buy you any kind of ice cream you want."

"I just have one question," said Simcha.

"No, I'm not buying you one also," snapped Menucha.

TWENTY

Binyamin awoke to the periodic ringing of his organizer's alarm, feeling slightly woozy. Binyamin had placed it on the bed table to make sure that he wouldn't miss its signal. He sat up, and the room spun crazily for a minute, leaving him with an unsettled nauseous feeling. No wonder, he thought, trying to remember his last meal. His schedule hadn't permitted regular meals, since he purposely crammed an inordinate amount of meetings into his days. He did this to utilize his time to its fullest so he could return as soon as possible to the kids.

Bleary-eyed, he focused on the jar of pickles he had left by his bedside. Not a good idea, he thought, as another wave of nauseous exhaustion hit him. Checking his organizer's schedule screen reminded him, despite his sleep-befuddled state, that he had to be at his next business meeting in forty-five minutes.

This wasn't just any business meeting, though. This meeting was with Bi Hai Shan, the head of one of the major pearl emporiums that Binyamin had been trying to establish business ties with for years. He had only succeeded in arranging this meeting through Herculean efforts over the past few weeks. It was a major stroke of good fortune, or at least he hoped it would be. But what he needed first was a shower. That would help him recover his equilibrium.

Seven minutes later, feeling worlds better, Binyamin stooped to place his wallet and organizer in a fresh pair of pants. His cell phone followed, though he paused as he noted the screen, which he realized he had not even glanced at earlier that morning. Did he have time to pick up a message? Not right now. It would only slow him down, and this meeting was too important to be late for. Deliberately, he placed the cell phone in his pocket, straightened his jacket and took a quick peek in the mirror. He was ready to go.

TWENTY-ONE

Nervously, Shira answered the summons of the door chimes.

"You're early," she said, after swinging the door open to the Eisenberg residence and quickly scanning the street for the sight of the three errant youngsters she had sent out a mere fifteen minutes before. She heaved a sigh of relief that no one was in sight.

"I just couldn't wait another minute," said the petite woman who stepped inside, eagerly surveying the front hall and every doorway in view.

"I asked you not to come," Shira said, restraining herself from reaching out to stop the woman as she picked up a gold-rimmed Lenox vase on the entrance table and studied it closely.

"I couldn't stay away," the woman said, moving over to peek into the dining room. "Lovely taste," she murmured admiringly.

"I thought I made it clear that the time wasn't right," Shira complained as the stylishly dressed woman turned right and left, patting her silver hair into place and taking in her full reflection and the reflection of everything else around her in the mirrored hallway. "What if they find out?"

"Where are they?" the woman asked, turning eagerly toward Shira. "I figured they would beat you to the door, but I don't even see them."

"They're out," said Shira, decidedly vague.

"Out?" the woman responded in surprise.

"Right," said Shira vehemently. "So why again did you come?"

"You know how it is with me."

"But you could ruin everything!" Shira exclaimed, her voice rising a decibel in her nervousness, which she quickly attempted to control. "I was just starting to make some headway, but if you keep interfering—"

"I'm *not* interfering," was the response. "I just came to see how you were getting along."

"I don't have time for this," said Shira, her tone almost pleading. "It isn't going to make my job any easier, you know, unless you just leave me alone to do what I have to do."

"That's your opinion," said the woman, "but being here is important to me. I needed to see you, and I needed to come here so I could feel closer to the whole thing. It makes me feel easier to be able to know what you're getting yourself involved in, in case you need advice or anything."

"Advice?" said Shira, her eyes searching for understanding. "Advice is great, but there's a time and place for everything. Please understand me. I really don't want to offend you in any way, but what's wrong with using the phone? Why are you insisting on doing this in person, and now of all times?"

"What better time than now?" said her visitor, with a smile.

Unconvinced, Shira just then happened to glance through the front window. To her dismay, she noticed the Eisenberg children across the street. "This can't be happening. The kids are coming back. What are they doing home?"

"They're here?" Shira's visitor whirled around. "Now?"

"Don't say a word," said Shira grimly. "If they figure out who you are, the whole game is up. This could ruin everything."

"Shira, this is crazy. Why can't I just meet them?"

"Please just pretend that everything's normal," said Shira, her breath coming in nervous gasps.

"It is," her visitor said calmly. "I can visit you. You'll just tell them I'm—"

"Who?" asked Shira. "How am I supposed to explain—"

"Just say I'm your mother."

"My mother!" said a wild-eyed Shira, her eyes narrowing as she took in her visitor in minute detail. "Oh, all right. I suppose I could just tell them that. I'm probably just panicking for no reason. What's wrong with my mother coming to visit after all?"

"Nothing," said the visitor dryly.

"Just don't get all gushy," Shira warned. "After all, they *aren't* your grandchildren."

"No, they're not, but I could always pretend. I've wanted

grandchildren for a long time, and this would be good for prac-tice, don't you think?"

"Okay," said Shira, ignoring the woman's sarcasm, "just don't let anything slip. Oh, how did I ever get myself into this? They are never going to believe—"

"What, that I'm your mother?" asked the woman. "Don't worry. I'll be the model of decorum." The woman looked out the front window at the three children coming towards the front door. "Oh, aren't they cute. The big girl looks like she could run this house single-handedly—just look at that expression, so adult-like and determined, and oh, that little girl is so cute. And I bet the boy is the model big brother. Look how he holds that little one's hand."

"I just want to know what they're doing here," said Shira, shaking her head. "I made arrangements. I had it all planned out. Why oh why are they making everything so hard for me?"

"Even the best of plans..." murmured the woman before swooshing open the door to greet the surprised threesome before they had even climbed the two steps to the front door. "Darlings! I'm so glad to meet you at long last."

TWENTY-TWO

The curtain fluttered gently closed as the old woman stood shaking her head in disgust. No sooner had the father gone, leaving that young woman in charge of things, when she was inviting her friends over. It was the same story all the time with help. You never could trust them. You'd think people would learn.

She had seen the babysitter's attempts at ridding herself of the children, her too cheerful goodbyes that signaled something more like good riddance, but the children had outsmarted her. They were back, and their sitter was clearly surprised. Her guest seemed to have recovered her composure well, but from where the old woman was standing—at her usual lookout post by the window—it was obvious that something was amiss. The babysitter was not happy that her charges had returned. She must have been planning some mischief. Hired help was always like that. Couldn't trust them with the silver, let alone your own children. Even if Mr. Eisenberg had gone away and left that young lady in charge, Mrs. Rosenman was going to be vigilant. That young upstart required watching. Something wasn't right over there, and someone had to keep an eye out for the children.

TWENTY-THREE

"Who are you?" Menucha asked, hesitating as she took in the stylishly dressed older woman in a navy, two-piece suit with gold braid, gold buttons and a nautical design.

"Just call me bubby," gushed the woman as she stepped towards the three hesitant children. "You're all as cute as a button."

Yocheved vigorously rubbed the cheek the older woman had just pinched. Simcha backed away as if expecting the same treatment. Only Menucha stood her ground.

"Whose bubby are you?" Menucha demanded, looking over at Shira as if expecting an answer.

"Meet my mother," said Shira brightly. "She came all this way to see you."

"Why?" Menucha asked pointedly. "She's not our bubby."

"We don't have a bubby," said Yocheved forlornly.

"Well, you can pretend you do now, sweetheart," said the professed bubby as she knelt to encircle Yocheved with her arms. "You are just too cute for words. I would love for you to be my granddaughter."

"Really?" asked Yocheved. "Everyone else in my class has a bubby, but I just have a grandma and a savta. Can I tell them that I have a bubby now, too?"

"Of course, you can," said the woman.

"No, you can't," said Menucha at the same time. "You can't just decide someone's your bubby. They have to be related."

"Well, Shira's our babysitter," said Yocheved, "and she said this is her mother so—"

"Babysitters aren't related," said Simcha matter-of-factly.

"And this is the boy," the woman continued to gush.

"Good guess," said Simcha with a half smile.

"It is, isn't it?" the woman said obliviously as she beamed her hundred-watt smile in Simcha's direction. "And you're the big girl."

"I am the biggest girl here," said Menucha, crossing her arms in front of her and glaring in her most belligerent and standoffish manner.

"Thrilled to meet you! Shira has told me so much about you."

"Well she hasn't told us a thing about you," said Menucha. "Like—"

"Let's not get all bogged down in details," said the older woman smoothly as she reached over once again to stroke

Yocheved's cheek. "Just call me Bubby, and that will be that."

"But you're not really our bubby," said Yocheved somewhat sadly.

"We can still pretend," said the alleged bubby, taking Yocheved's hand. "Come show me your room, and your toys. I would love to get to know you better."

"Why?" Menucha asked to Yocheved's rapidly retreating back.

"That's just how my mother is," said Shira, helplessly watching the older woman and Yocheved leave the room. "I'll go make sure she stays out of trouble. But, Menucha, after she leaves you are going to have a lot of explaining to do, like exactly why you came home after I made a play date for all of you."

Shira rushed out of the room after the pair as if her life depended on it.

"A *play date!*" shrieked Menucha in disgust. "Like we're all seven years old like Yocheved and need to have our friends arranged for us— What are you doing, Simcha? You know better than to touch things that don't belong to you."

"Sorry," said Simcha jumping guiltily away from the older woman's pocketbook that he had been about to open. "I was just—"

"You were just stooping to Shira's level," said Menucha with righteous indignation.

"Well, yeah," said Simcha. "Why not? How else are we supposed to protect ourselves?"

"By going through her pocketbook?" Menucha said. "What's that supposed to do for us?"

"Well, she did leave it here," said Simcha pointedly.

"So what? Shows that she trusts us, even if I don't trust her."

"Do you think she's really Shira's mother?" asked Simcha.

"She sure doesn't look like Shira," said Menucha thoughtfully. "Shira is more petite, and her hair is lighter and her eyes are green. This lady is fatter, and her eyes are brown, and her hair is darker and curlier, though I suppose she could be the right age."

"Maybe she's wearing a *sheitel*," said Simcha.

"Who cares if it is or it isn't Shira's mother," said Menucha. "Besides, if she's a spy, they all wear wigs anyway. It's part of their disguise. Anyway, the fact is that she still looks nothing like Shira."

"I know how to find out who she really is!" said Simcha smugly.

"How?" asked Menucha.

"Like this," said Simcha, stepping forward after a surreptitious glance around the room.

This time Menucha didn't stop him when he lifted the flap of the heavily perfumed, brown leather handbag and reached inside the yawning pocket. After another hasty glance around, he unsnapped the maroon leather billfold he had removed and found what he was looking for.

"She lied," said Menucha matter-of-factly as she leaned over Simcha's shoulder to survey the driver's license. "I knew it."

"Seems so," said Simcha as he hastily replaced the wallet. He heard sounds coming towards him down the hall. "Shirley B. Lelchook is certainly no relation to our Shira Baum, unless one of them is lying about their last name, and even if one is, why would they, unless they had something to hide?"

TWENTY-FOUR

"I just can't decide," said a troubled voice. "I thought maybe you could help me."

"I can try," said the older voice, surprised by the request. "It's been a long time since someone asked me for help."

"But I really need your help now," said the other. "He'll be back soon and I have to decide before he comes home."

"There will be trouble," said the older voice, "once he sees what's going on around here."

"Why?" asked the first.

"Never you mind, just mark my words. When do you have to be back?"

"Oh, no one will miss me," was the reply. "They're all busy with other things right now."

"I don't need any trouble," said the elder, setting down a tray of orange tea biscuits and two glasses of lemonade. "I'll just look over these papers, and you can come back another day. Then we'll decide exactly what's best for you. He won't be back that soon, will he?"

"I don't think so."

"Good, then when you're finished with the lemonade, you just come back any time after today."

"Thanks. No one else would even think of asking you. They're all scared of you, but I knew you could help me."

"Scared of me?" There was surprise in the old voice. "Well, I hope I can help," murmured the older voice, as clawed fingers reached out to touch the pages that would have to be looked over bit by bit before any advice at all could be offered.

TWENTY-FIVE

"What did you do with that woman?" Menucha cornered her little sister in her room as soon as Shira had followed her alleged mother out the door and to her car. Simcha "just happened" to mosey after the pair in case they wanted to exchange any information or otherwise do something that his presence would prevent.

"You mean Bubby?" Yocheved asked.

"She's *not* your bubby!" said Menucha. "But yes, that's who I mean."

"I showed her the projects I made in camp," Yocheved said. "I showed her my room."

"What else?" Menucha pressed.

"Why?" asked Yocheved suspiciously. "How come you don't like her?"

"I didn't say I don't like her," said Menucha.

"You don't have to say it," said Yocheved. "You don't like anybody, not Shira, not Bubby—"

"She's *not* your bubby!" said Menucha.

"I can call her what I want to call her and you can't stop me!" said Yocheved, flouncing over to her bed and plunking herself down, wrinkling the smooth lacy, lilac patterned comforter and bouncing so hard that she nearly bumped her head into the shelf of stuffed animals that was on the wall above her headboard. She picked up Baila Chana from beside her and held her tight for moral support. "You're just being mean because you don't like her."

"Okay," said Menucha, "you're right. I don't like her."

"Well, I do like her," said Yocheved. "I always wanted a bubby."

"For the millionth time, she's not your bubby," said Menucha, gritting her teeth in frustration.

"Well, she said she is," said Yocheved, inserting her thumb stubbornly into her mouth as if to put an end to the conversation.

"Someday you'll learn," Menucha said, looking down at her little sister with a look akin to pity, "that family—real family—always comes first."

TWENTY-SIX

"We have to get our hands on those plans for the new line of water pearl jewelry already," the gruff voice cracked with impatience. "We need to begin work on it now, and with him not around, we have to get moving before it's too late. Everything rests on us getting a hold of those plans and starting to work now. It's absolutely ridiculous that you can't find them. He undoubtedly left them in that house *somewhere*. I can't believe he would leave them just lying around, but check every single room. This is getting ridiculous already!"

"Well, don't blame me!" said Shira, pulling the laundry room door shut behind her for more privacy. "I've looked everywhere."

"If you had really looked everywhere, then you would have found them."

"Don't give me any of that," said Shira. "Maybe they're in his office at work. Did you think of looking there?"

"Now, that's a possibility. I doubt it, but maybe. That's the only other reasonable idea, but I still have a feeling that they're in his house. I'll have his office at work searched. I can do that tonight. In the meantime, don't give up looking in his house. If they're not locked up in his filing cabinet like you claim, then he could have left them anywhere."

"We'll find them," she soothed him. "Don't worry."

"Don't worry, she tells me, like I can do anything else. How can I not worry, and what about you? It's your job on the line, too, I'll warrant. You might think you're sitting pretty over there, but without those plans who knows what could happen."

"I'm not worried," said Shira coldly. "I think I have more going for me than just this right now."

"I wouldn't count on it," he said, his tone as desperate as a drowning man clutching desperately at whatever straws he could pull down into the whirlpool with him.

TWENTY-SEVEN

Thursday afternoon, July 8 — China

Having met with Bi Hai Shan, Binyamin was feeling positively euphoric. If only all of his plans for this trip would work out so successfully. Though nothing had been finalized, the details that they had discussed today in Bi Hai Shan's office were enough to give Binyamin big hopes for the new line of freshwater pearl jewelry he hoped to create soon through all of the contacts he was working on now.

Bi Hai Shan had invited Binyamin to dinner tonight. An invitation to dinner, Binyamin mused, was a singularly big honor, too big of an honor to refuse despite the fact that Binyamin wouldn't be eating a bite of it. He hoped Bi Hai Shan wouldn't mind. Probably his host wouldn't even notice, given the size of the affairs that Binyamin had already heard were frequently given for his business associates.

Leaning back in the cracked upholstered seat of the taxi, Binyamin closed his eyes as a wave of exhaustion overcame him. Crossing his arms, his hand brushed against the shape of his cell phone in his pocket, which reminded him of the message that he had left untouched earlier. Retrieving the phone from his pocket, Binyamin put the phone to his ear and listened.

Instantly overcome with guilt, Binyamin dialed with fingers suddenly gone clumsy in nervousness, as he mentally berated himself over and over for having ignored the message for this long.

TWENTY-EIGHT

"Hello," said Shira, her voice thick with sleep.

"Shira," said Binyamin. "What's going on?"

"Going on?" said Shira, waking up with a start when she realized who she had on the line. "What's supposed to be going on? Is everything okay with you?"

"With me!" said Binyamin. "I just got this message from Menucha who said—oh, never mind. Forget what she said. Just tell me, is everything okay with you and the kids?"

"I think so," said Shira. "I mean I haven't checked on them for the past few hours—"

"You haven't checked on them?" said Binyamin his voice near panic. "Why not?"

"It's 4 a.m. for one thing," said Shira, holding the cordless phone with her shoulder as she slipped into her robe. "I don't think anything much has happened since we all went to bed."

"I'm sorry about the time, Shira," said a chagrined Binyamin. "I guess I totally panicked. I completely forgot the time difference there. Just peek in on the kids, will you, and tell me that they're okay."

"Not a problem," said Shira. "I was on my way."

Shira padded silently down the hall, peering into the first bedroom. Yocheved slept peacefully, her thumb tucked securely into her mouth, her cheeks pink and cherubic in the soft glow of the nightlight beside her bed.

"Yocheved's fine," said Shira, peeking into Simcha's room next. "Simcha is also sound asleep."

Silently, she turned the knob of Menucha's room.

"Who's there?" asked Menucha, sitting bolt up right in bed, startled from sleep by the squeak of the door on its hinges.

"Only me," said Shira. "I was just checking on you."

"With the phone?" asked Menucha, staring suspiciously at Shira silhouetted in her doorway with the light in the hall behind her.

"I was talking to your father," said Shira.

"She's up?" Binyamin said. "Let me talk to her."

"Sure," said Shira, passing the phone over to Menucha.

"Hi, Tatti," said Menucha cheerfully, babbling on though her father had yet to get a word in edgewise. "That file that Simcha found. It was nothing important, just some old catalogues. What? Oh, good idea. I also think Shira should go back to sleep. It's too bad you had to wake her up."

Shira hesitated in the doorway, still unsure if whatever Binyamin had called about had been resolved, but from the look Menucha was giving her, it was only too clear that she wasn't welcome here. Shira left.

"Ta?" said Menucha after hearing the click of Shira's door further down the hall.

"What was that all about?" her father asked her. "Is it okay if I speak now?"

"I just couldn't have her standing here," said Menucha. "I have to talk to you!"

"What's the meaning of all this is what I want to know," Binyamin said. "You scared me half to death with that message of yours. Shira says everything is fine."

"She would," huffed Menucha. "Tatti, you have to come home."

"Oh, Menucha," sighed her father. "Is that was this is all about? You did this to me the last time I went away also. I am not coming home, despite your attempts at being melodramatic. I'm happy to hear there are no real life and death issues you need me for, and so, on that note, I'll—"

"Tatti," Menucha interrupted, "it's not just because I want you to come home. I mean I do, but I understand you have work. But you're going to *need* to come home and fast."

"Why?" asked Binyamin. "You know I'll get there as soon as I can. I don't like being away any more than you. I've left you in perfectly capable hands, and you need to accept that."

"Ta," Menucha said. "Shira's a spy."

"A what?" her father exclaimed.

"A spy," said Menucha.

"Is that your life and death issue then?" asked her father, annoyance clear in his voice. "I must admit it's creative, but it isn't going to work. I'm not coming home."

"I have proof," said Menucha.

"Oh yeah, what?" asked her father with a sigh of resignation.

"She knew all about Simcha's allergy to nuts," said Menucha triumphantly. "It means she researched everything about us. She knew our favorite kind of pizza, she knew what kind of music CD to get us, sh—"

"Menucha," her father's voice was grim and icy. "I think you need to calm down. Shira is not a spy. I told her about your brother's nut allergies. His allergies are serious. He blows up like a balloon if he so much as gets near a nut. Do you really think I would have a sitter in the house and *not* tell her about that?"

"But, Ta," said Menucha, ignoring the niggling thought that she had been wrong on the nut theory in her rush to prove herself further, "there's more! When I came home from camp one day, I wasn't supposed to be home, but I was, and when I went past the window to your study, I saw Shira opening up all your files and faxing them t—"

"You were peeking into windows when Shira didn't know you were there?" Binyamin said.

"Well, I guess so," said Menucha, "but it's a good thing I was because—"

"You are the spy, young lady," said Binyamin. "I can't believe a daughter of mine would go skulking around the house to spy on someone."

"But Tatti," wailed Menucha, "she was looking through your—"

"I'm hanging up now, Menucha," said her father. "I love you very much. I know you miss me, but you're just going to have to take my word for it. Shira is *not* a spy. I give you my word."

"Tatti, it's your business she's after!" said Menucha her frantic tone arresting her father. "I know it. Just yesterday, this lady came over. She pretended she was Shira's mother, but I know better. She was some contact of hers. Shira is here to steal your jewelry designs! I know it!"

"Shira works for me," said Binyamin. "Why would she steal designs from her own company?"

"I can't explain that to you," said Menucha, "but you have to believe me, she—"

"And you have to believe me," said Binyamin. "Shira is not a spy. I refuse to hear any more about this. I want you to get along with Shira, to help her and to make her job easier. I trust Shira completely. That should be enough for you."

"But Tatti!" Menucha said. "You're not listening!"

"Menucha," said Binyamin. "I have to go. My taxi is pulling up to the hotel. Think it over. I won't say a word about this to Shira, if you don't say another word about it to me. Got it?"

"But—"

"Got it?" her father said again.

"What else can I say?" asked a frustrated Menucha.

"How about good night?" her father said.

"Good night, Tatti," said Menucha, "but you're making a big mist—"

A dial tone met her last words. Her father had already hung up.

TWENTY-NINE

Binyamin was once again in the back of a taxi, but this time he was heading out of Beijing towards his dinner date. The drive was long, but he hoped he had managed to calculate a timely arrival. He unfolded himself from the back seat of the taxi after paying his driver. The ride had been pleasant enough, once they had gotten beyond the confines of the city where the chaos from the incredible numbers of people, bikes, taxis and buses had been more than a bit overwhelming. It was a pleasure to have left all of that behind and to step out into the comfortably cool evening with just a hint of a breeze.

With keen interest, he studied the address he had arrived at. Amazingly enough, before him stood a house, a rarity in

China, which was so densely populated that almost everyone in the cities, or anywhere near the major cities, lived in apartments. The amount of land around the house only further attested to the financial status he had heard that his host held. A long stone wall on all sides mostly concealed the house, but it was hard to make out its exact features in the weak light of early evening.

Binyamin passed hesitantly through the gateway and approached the impressive receded, arched doorway. Nervously, he straightened his tie and jacket and headed up the walkway paved with granite flagging and edged with delicate garden plants, including a tinkling fountain that straddled a tiny stream of clear water ending in a pond filled with flowering lily pads and overgrown goldfish. Binyamin paused momentarily when a bright orange and black Koi fish surfaced, its mouth gaping as if begging for some choice tidbit.

Approaching the door, Binyamin checked his watch. Either he was incredibly late, or he had the wrong date or time. Everything seemed too quiet for the large dinner party that Bi Hai Shan had described. There was only one way to find out, though. Binyamin raised the doorknocker twisted into the shape of a flaming dragon, and winced as the heavy thud resounded through the rich mahogany of the ornately carved door.

Seconds later, a petite Chinese woman stood in the doorway before him. She bowed her head. Binyamin inclined his head as well in order to be polite and also in order to hide his surprise. Rather than the evening clothes or at the very least a rich kimono that would have fit so well into the oriental surroundings, this woman was wearing what could only be described as silk pajamas.

Now, Binyamin knew he had made this mistake before. How many times had he complimented one or the other of his daughters on her lovely Shabbos dress only to have her break off into peals of laughter that would eventually subside into an explanation that the garb she was attired in was not a dress but a Shabbos robe?

The outfit before him could not be mistaken though. It was not a Shabbos robe, but was clearly a pair of gold pinstriped pajamas, made from the finest silk material obviously, but pajamas nonetheless.

"I'm so sorry for having disturbed you," Binyamin said, hoping against hope that this woman understood English as he turned momentarily in the vain hope that he would be able to glimpse the cab had brought him. "I was under the impression that this was Bi Hai Shan's house and that he was hosting a dinner for this evening. I am so sorry for having disrupted your rest."

"No, no, not disturbing," the woman said in heavily accented English, her porcelain features solemn.

"But you're getting ready to go to sleep," Binyamin protested in embarrassment. "I must have gotten the time wrong."

"Not wrong. Party here. Bi Hai Shan home now. Guests in back. Come."

Mystified, Binyamin relented as the little woman beckoned Binyamin inside but halted in confusion when she held out a hand to stop his progress.

"Please remove," she told him politely, pointing to the dark mat beside the door on which two pairs of shoes already rested, further proof that Binyamin had the wrong house, because if a party was going on inside, where were the shoes of all the other partygoers?

"Of course," Binyamin said, ready to kick himself for not remembering the Chinese custom of removing shoes before entering the house. Chagrined, he took the pair of slippers that he was offered and again tried to proceed.

"Take," she commanded simply as Binyamin again was stopped from stepping forward by the tiny woman blocking his entry.

"What?" he asked looking around wildly, wondering what was coming next.

"Shoes," she said simply.

Confused, Binyamin took up his shoes and followed the petite woman as he was ushered through the house. He walked past Ming furniture and ornate, massive vases made of cloisonné enamel in stunning shades of pale green and white against a background of peacock blue and gilded with gold. Lacquered paper partitions decorated with Chinese calligraphy and delicately brushed sprigs of flowers divided one room from another and rich embroidered tapestries hung on the walls beside dainty, unframed Chinese scrolls. The thick carpet he caught a glimpse of as he passed one of the rooms he was sure was a handmade Baihua carpet with a phoenix design woven among the plum blossom pattern.

Binyamin was so entranced with his surroundings that he

nearly bumped into his guide as she stood by a sliding door exchanging her slippers for shoes. Binyamin followed suit, leaving his slippers on the mat beside the door as he changed into his shoes and stepped outside into a lush garden suffused with the perfume of various planted flowers. Binyamin realized, both from the number of people and the small garden tables set out and peppered with eager diners, that there was indeed a party going on there that night.

"Ah, Mr. Eisenberg," Bi Hai Shan said as he emerged from a group of people and hurried forward to greet his guest. "So glad you could make it!"

"Thank you," said Binyamin, shaking hands with Bi Hai Shan and hoping that his sweaty palms would be undetectable.

"I see you've met my wife, Li Wei," Bi Hai Shan nodded towards the woman who had walked with Binyamin through the house. "We are immensely pleased to have you tonight at this special occasion."

"I thank you so much for the invitation," said Binyamin. "I'm just sorry that your wife doesn't seem to be feeling well."

"Not feeling well?" said Bi Hai Shan in astonishment. "Li Wei, you are not well?"

His wife responded in a short spurt of tinkling Chinese.

"My wife says to tell you that she is quite well," said Bi Hai Shan.

"I'm happy to hear that," said Binyamin uncomfortably. "I just assumed—"

"Assumed what?" Bi Hai Shan pressed.

"That I was disturbing her rest," said Binyamin, looking over again at the gold colored pajamas with the black stripes running through them.

"Ah, I see," said Bi Hai Shan with a barely concealed smile. "Come, meet the rest of my guests."

Binyamin was ushered forward and introduced to many of Bi Hai Shan's guests. Binyamin found the whole scene strangely discomfiting. What kind of party had he been invited to anyway? Though the men, business associates of Bi Hai Shan were dressed in jackets and ties like Binyamin, most of the woman, at least the Chinese women were dressed in various garbs of sleepwear, which served to only further confuse Binyamin and make him wonder exactly what kind of a party had he gotten himself into.

"I was told it is not the custom in America," his host observed.

"What is not?" asked Binyamin, trying to be the perfect guest and hoping his face gave away nothing of what he was feeling.

"Here in China," Bi Hai Shan stated, "silk pajamas are regarded as a sign of wealth and prestige. It's quite appropriate to wear them out shopping, let's say, or to visit friends. Though I prefer my business associates to not be able to completely relax in my presence, my wife encourages their wives to come as they please so that she can wear her own silk pajamas."

"I see," said Binyamin weakly, though he didn't see at all.

"Understand," said his host, "that it was not so long ago that many of the Chinese people owned nothing more than one suit of clothes. To be able to afford pajamas today is the sign of the luxurious times in which we live, and its comfort speaks for itself."

"That I can understand," said Binyamin, vowing not to tell his kids about this prevalent custom. It was often hard enough to insist that they get dressed on the days they had off from school, as they too seemed to agree that pajamas or robes were more comfortable than more conventional clothes.

"Something to eat, Mr. Eisenberg?" his hostess inquired, appearing at his elbow.

"Ah, yes, you are in for some extraordinary Chinese delicacies," said Bi Hai Shan leading him around a fringe of trees. The aroma of roasting meat became stronger as they approached a brightly-lit pavilion. "You will make your selection, and it will be prepared for you."

"I really don't—" Binyamin began to explain himself out of his predicament but Bi Hai Shan's attention was elsewhere. With a snap of his fingers, Bi Hai Shan beckoned towards one of the white hatted, aproned men. The servant came forward immediately, and after a few rapid fire Chinese words seemed to have been permanently assigned to Binyamin's elbow.

"If you'll excuse me," Bi Hai Shan said, before melting into the crowd. "This boy understands some English so he will make himself most useful."

Out of sheer curiosity, Binyamin stepped towards the numerous loaded tables in front of him, noting that the servants seemed to be cooking and carrying the food over to different areas in the gardens for their guests.

"What on earth?" Binyamin exclaimed.

The Chinese servant at his elbow jumped back several paces as other people looked disapprovingly over at Binyamin.

"What's that?" Binyamin asked, pointing to the cages of animals on a side table.

"Ah, very good, you want?" his servant asked, nodding vigorously and going forward to unlatch the cage.

"No, thank you," Binyamin said hastily, as a vague, sickening notion began to tickle the corners of his mind. "I don't want, but what is it?"

"This, civet cat," his shadow told him, nodding sagely at the furry creature. "Excellent with right sauce. I make right sauce. No problem."

"Actually, yes, problem," said Binyamin, beginning to break out in a cold sweat as he surveyed the tables before him.

Rather than ready cooked foods, salads and other miscellaneous, Binyamin spied a whole conglomeration of foods, fresh foods, very fresh foods—too fresh. Beside the cage of the civet cat rested a cage filled with what could only be rattlesnakes. Binyamin had heard that the upper class and other Chinese ate snakes and assorted other animals, but he hadn't really given it much thought until today. A peacock strutted in a pen behind the tables loaded with cages. Was that to eat too? Surrounding it were the more mundane and familiar, ducks and chickens, and possibly a turkey. Binyamin couldn't believe his eyes when a young servant, similar in appearance to his own, chased after a rather heavy white goose, hatchet in hand, his intentions only too clear to all, including the loudly honking goose.

Beside the snakes was a cage that appeared empty, but upon closer inspection, Binyamin noted the occupants hanging upside down, or right side up for them. A thick shadow of bats clung to the roof of their cage, sound asleep and oblivious to their fate should someone select them as their meal of choice.

A fox stared out of his cramped quarters as Binyamin passed, its bright eyes sharp with worry. In the pen behind it a fat boar rooted around beside a thick puddle of mud that it soon settled back into with a sigh. All around him, guests were selecting their meals and servants were hurrying off to prepare their fresh delicacies. A cage of white furry rabbits particularly tugged at Binyamin's heart. Even if he found a whole fruit, there was no way Binyamin was going to eat it now. He also noted a lobster that was trying to crawl out of the huge silver pan it was resting in, while crabs lurked at the bottom of the dish near a glass aquarium of huge fish not unlike the Koi's he had seen outside.

"You no like?" Binyamin's servant asked worriedly from his elbow, pointing towards the jumbo shrimp in the silver basin nearest them on the table.

"I'll pass, I think, thank you."

"I get special food for you," said the servant worriedly. "Dragon and tiger head, special dish. You see."

"What's in it?" Binyamin asked, his curiosity getting the better of him.

"Special Chinese secret," said the servant with a wink, "secret being mostly snake and cat, special seasonings, too. You like?"

"No, thank you," Binyamin declared forcefully, turning his back on the whole menagerie.

"Special for honored guest," said Li Wei materializing out of the smoke from the many open fires that were drifting in their direction.

Binyamin's servant took the plate and offered it to Binyamin as Li Wei hurried off to attend to more of her guests.

"Ah, very good," he sighed sniffing the aroma ecstatically, "is pangolin dish."

"Whatever it is," said Binyamin forcefully, "I don't want it."

"Here you take it," said the servant, nervously thrusting the dish at Binyamin. "Rude to hostess if you refuse to take."

Binyamin found himself staring down at a plate full of small chunks of meat swimming in a brown sauce. Not knowing what to do with the plate, he backed out of the pavilion and found himself on a narrow path leading towards a bridge. Wondering if it was the same stream that trickled past the front of the house, Binyamin approached the delicately arched bridge and studied the water. A pond similar to the one in the front yard reflected the full moon above him and the Chinese lanterns on the path beside him. The surface was broken here and there by the fins of one of the gigantic Koi, and occasionally by a hungry mouth breaking the surface. Binyamin had an idea. Not wanting to touch the meat on his plate, Binyamin bent to find a twig, not an easy task in the perfectly manicured garden, but by the pond's edge, he found one. One by one he speared the bits of meat and tossed them into the pond, watching in amazement as the water boiled around each piece he threw in as the hungry fish converged upon it. Within seconds, his meat was gone. Taking the empty plate in his hands, a relieved Binyamin leaned against a sturdy stone pole, two of which flanked the bridge on either side.

"Ah, there you are!" said Bi Hai Shan, "being kept safe by the terra cotta soldiers of Xian."

"What?" asked a startled Binyamin, twisting around to study the "pole" he had been leaning on. It was indeed a life size statue of a Xian soldier that Binyamin had only noticed in much smaller sizes in the stores and gift shops he had visited on previous occasions.

"Amazing piece of work," Binyamin stuttered, looking up into the strangely distorted features of the stone piece that had supported him only moments before, but which he was loath to touch now that he knew what it was. "This whole place is like walking through a museum. You have some amazing works of art in the house as well."

"Thank you," his host nodded politely. "I do like to surround myself with beauty. It is restful for the spirit."

"Right," said Binyamin uncomfortably.

"I see you have been enjoying my specialty items," Bi Hai Shan nodded towards the plate Binyamin still held. "Tell me, what did you select, the badger perhaps, incredibly unique and special?"

"Actually," said Binyamin, overcome by the foreignness of it all, "I must admit that I didn't eat any of it. I do appreciate your kind invitation, but as an Orthodox Jew, I really can't eat any of these foods. I appreciate it nonetheless, and couldn't insult your wife by not accepting this dish as she served me, but I had to feed it to the fish. I personally can't eat such things. I eat only kosher, you see. Even though I have many dietary prohibitions, I didn't want to offend you by not accepting your invitation tonight, since, as you know, I am extremely interested in doing business with you."

"I see," said Bi Hai Shan, smiling broadly. "I was worried when my servant told me that he hadn't been able to tempt you with any of our dishes. It is not a good sign for business partners to not break bread together. But I understand you now to be a man of principles. It is a quality I do admire. Coming to my home exclusively for my honor and not for the glory of this meal, now that is something I respect. We will do well, you and I, Mr. Eisenberg. I foresee a long and pleasant business arrangement for the both of us. You will come to my office tomorrow, and we will work out more of the details. I will be honored to supply you with what you desire. Pearls, jade, gems—you have but to ask. But for now, come, surely there is some food items that I can provide you. A guest must not leave my home hungry. What exactly do you eat? I have a rich assortment of fruit. I will have it brought to you."

Binyamin couldn't believe his good fortune. Simply by being as straightforward as possible, unbelievable doors had opened to him. It was worth the whole harrowing night to have earned the respect of someone like Bi Hai Shan. The benefits to Binyamin's jewelry business were sure to be immeasurable.

THIRTY

Motzei Shabbos, July 10

"Menucha," said Shira, "do you mind getting that? I can't imagine who could be at the door at this hour of the night."

"Who is it?" Menucha called. After hearing the reply, she slowly opened the door.

Menucha was none too pleased to find herself nearly bowled over as her neighbor, Mrs. Rosenman, barreled past her and headed straight for the kitchen.

"Can I help you?" asked Shira, lifting her hands, sudsy with dishwater, from the sink. She took in the slight form of this rather eccentric looking woman. She was wearing a faded model's coat with wildflower motif, disheveled *tichel* and flapping pink house slippers.

"I should hope so," said Mrs. Rosenman with a sniff as she surveyed the wreckage of the kitchen that one Shabbos and three kids had managed to create in the normally well-kept house. "Tomorrow is my granddaughter's birthday. She's turning three, angelic little thing, and is so darling. I'm making her a party, though I suppose it's rather last minute to invite guests."

"That's lovely!" said Shira, "But we already have plans. I'm so sorry."

"What do you mean?" asked Mrs. Rosenman, confused.

"Tomorrow, your party," said Shira. "I'm afraid we won't be able to attend."

"I wasn't thinking of inviting you," said Mrs. Rosenman disdainfully. "I was thinking more on the lines of hired help."

"I beg your pardon?" said Shira, her cheeks suddenly turning as red as her hands.

"Hired help," Mrs. Rosenman repeated. "I suppose you're too busy with this job here," she said, as her nervous glance fluttered over the threesome, who were sitting wide eyed at the kitchen table taking in the whole scene. "But you must have some friends. I could use a waiter, I suppose. Also someone to serve and tidy up the house beforehand and clean up the garbage during the party, not to mention, of course, setting up, you know."

"No, I'm afraid I *don't* know," said Shira, her tone icy.

"Well," said Mrs. Rosenman, looking around the kitchen disdainfully, "that's rather obvious from the mess this place is in."

"Can I help you with something?" Shira asked, advancing on her unwelcome guest.

"I came to borrow something."

"Borrow?" Shira spluttered.

Shira looked to Menucha. "She's our neighbor," Menucha explained, embarrassed to have to admit any relationship at all to Mrs. Rosenman, who was treating Shira rather badly. As much as Menucha suspected Shira, she did not think that Shira deserved to be treated this way

"That's right, young lady. I'm a close neighbor of your boss," said Mrs. Rosenman, "so please don't get uppity with me. I happen to be keeping an eye on you, and I'm on extremely good terms with Mr. Eisenberg, so don't you get all hoity-toity with me. It's just as well that you don't know anyone for hire. It's always such a strain to keep an eye on them, and regardless the silver manages to slip out the door."

"What do you want to borrow?" asked Yocheved.

"Mr. Eisenberg's platter, the one with the pink and green tinted glass. Shouldn't these kids be in bed already?"

"I allowed them to stay up later tonight," said Shira coldly.

"So I see," said Mrs. Rosenman. "Mr. Eisenberg is terribly strict about bedtimes, I'll have you know. I'm sure he wouldn't approve of this."

"Maybe not," said Shira, "but excuse me, Mrs. Rosenman, it seems to me that you are keeping us all here. We still have some things to do."

"Like cleaning up perhaps?" said Mrs. Rosenman pointedly as she looked towards the kitchen table still covered with the debris of *shalosh seudos*, plus the remains of the board game that they had been playing before Shabbos ended.

"I keep a *very* clean house," said Shira. "It just so happens that you've caught me at a bad moment. Now if it's the platter you're after, I believe it's right in the dishwasher. I'll wash it myself for you, and you can take it right—"

Shira bent to open the dishwasher but hastily slammed the door shut, locked the latch and turned around with a strange expression on her face.

"The platter," Mrs. Rosenman reminded, taking a step forward as Shira hastily put herself in front of the dishwasher as if to protect its contents. "Is it in there?"

"In there?" asked Shira with a nervous laugh.

"Yes," said Mrs. Rosenman. "I was hoping to bring it home with me tonight to have ready in the morning."

"Don't you worry about a thing," said Shira, stepping forward and placing both of her hands on the little lady's shoulders. "I'll have it over for you early in the morning if not later tonight. I just couldn't send you home with a dish as dirty as that one."

"I thought you were going to wash it."

"Wash it? By hand?" said Shira incredulously. "Don't be silly. The dishwasher will do a much more reliable job. Washing dishes by hand is just not my strong point."

"I see," said Mrs. Rosenman. "What exactly are your strong points then?"

"Now that's a good question," said Shira, her voice still sounding higher and faster than normal as she propelled Mrs. Rosenman down the hall and out the front door. "I'll think of an answer and let you know first thing tomorrow when I bring over that platter. You have a wonderful night, now. Thank you so much for coming! And mazel tov on that birthday party tomorrow."

Mrs. Rosenman was out the door before she knew what had hit her. Shira hastily locked the door and shot the deadbolt in place for good measure.

"Don't ever let that woman back in this house without giving me at least three days warning," she said to the three kids who were now assembled in front of her. "Ever."

"Why not?" asked Yocheved.

"Come with me," said Shira, her commanding tone ringing shrill.

Shira approached the dishwasher and slowly, gingerly lowered the door. Three pairs of curious eyes leaned over to survey the contents.

"Yuck!" screamed Yocheved.

"Yuck! Please close it," Menucha begged.

"That is soooo gross," Simcha said, almost retching at the sight of a dishwasher teeming with fat, black carpenter ants swarming over the plates, silverware and other miscellaneous dishes that were piled inside, still dirty from the Shabbos table, making them especially attractive to their unwelcome visitors.

"No wonder you didn't want to loan her that platter!" said Menucha, for once agreeing with Shira. "Not that she really needed it. She's always coming over to borrow things she doesn't need."

"But maybe she really did need it for her party," Yocheved insisted stoutly.

"Maybe," said Shira, "but I think something needs to be done about a neighbor like that."

Menucha and Simcha widened their eyes. Was Shira not only a spy but possibly violent as well?

"Like what?" asked a curious Yocheved.

"I'll think of something," said Shira.

"But what are you going to do with all those ants?" Yocheved asked.

"There's only one answer," said Shira, reaching over to press the right button.

With a rush of water and a swoosh of power, the dishwasher was all set to wash dirt, debris and ants all down the drain.

"You forgot the soap," Yocheved pointed out.

"We'll run it again later," said Shira, "once the ants are all gone."

"Now can we get an exterminator?" Menucha asked.

"Now we can get an exterminator," Shira agreed. "I am never, ever going through such a mortifying scene again in my life. Don't you dare tell anyone else about this! I'll never live it down."

"By the way," Simcha said thoughtfully as the dishwasher surged and gushed. "Are ants kosher?"

"Why?" Menucha asked. "Do you want to eat one? Maybe Tatti can bring you home some that are chocolate covered if you ask nicely."

"No, thanks," said Simcha, smirking. "I was just wondering about the dishes. They can get awfully hot in a dishwasher with all that hot water, and isn't it kind of like you're cooking the ants there with all those dishes?"

Shira's eyes widened in horror as she realized the enormity of her mistake.

"Tatti's not going to be happy if our Shabbos dishes aren't kosher any more," Menucha said. "Remember when I broke that little bowl and Tatti explained to us how these dishes were irreplaceable? He got them from some foreign country or other on one of his trips years ago."

"And you can't *kasher* china, can you?" Simcha said thoughtfully.

"We'll have to ask a rav," Shira said in a strangled tone.

"Is this still going to be a secret?" Yocheved asked innocently, but no one answered. All eyes were too busy staring at the dishwasher as the full ramifications of pressing that one little button hit home.

THIRTY-ONE

"We should have done all this stuff last night," Menucha said critically as she came down the stairs to add her beach bag to the pile of gear that had already been heaped into the front hall to be taken out to the car. "At this rate, we're never going to get an early start. You'd think that an adult would realize this!"

"It's plenty early," Simcha said as he came down and added his own things: fishing rod, binoculars, bat, ball and kite to the ever-growing mound. "Shira woke me up at seven o'clock. I couldn't believe it."

"It's already after eight," said Menucha pointedly. "Did you find the sunscreen yet?"

"I don't know where it is," said Simcha.

"We're not leaving without sunscreen," Menucha said.

"I think we used it all up last year," said Simcha as Shira came pounding down the stairs fresh out of the shower, the shoulders of her shirt damp from her dripping wet hair. Her bare feet left watery footprints on the wood stairs.

"We can't find the sunscreen, Shira," Menucha said. "We'll have to go out and buy some before we go."

"Yocheved?" Shira called up the stairs as she knotted the belt on her long, denim skirt. "Do you know where the sunscreen is?"

"Yes," Yocheved answered.

There was the sound of the upstairs linen closet being tugged open and moments later Yocheved appeared with a white tube in her hand.

"Good girl," said Shira, smiling triumphantly. "Now we won't have to go shopping before we set off. Come put some on me now so that it has time to soak in before we get to White Lake. I'll do you next."

Yocheved stood on the third step to be able to reach Shira's face to spread on the cream. She started applying the sunscreen, and then paused abruptly. "Are you sure Mr. and Mrs. Walberg said we could come to their lake house?" she asked Shira. "Even if Tatti's not home?"

"They really want us to come," Shira said, "probably *because* your Tatti's not home, and they know how much you guys miss your father."

"How do you know the Walbergs?" Menucha asked.

"I know Mr. Walberg is your father's business partner," said

Shira, "and I know he and his wife invite you guys to their house in White Lake at least once each summer."

"Is he going to let us go in the motor boat?" Yocheved asked.

"Of course," said Shira, "if you wear a life jacket."

"I can swim," said Yocheved.

"So can I," said Shira, "and I'll be wearing one, too. We can go in the rowboat, too, if you want."

"Rowboat?" Yocheved asked, beginning to sing *Row, Row, Row Your Boat*.

"Right, and the canoe," said Shira, wrinkling her nose to test the cream Yocheved had smeared on it. "This stuff is awfully thick. How old is it?"

"Rub it in better," Menucha told Yocheved, as Shira's face became a mask of white.

"I am rubbing," said Yocheved between stanzas of her song. "I guess that's just how this looks."

"It sure smells strange," said Simcha, wrinkling his own nose as he approached the foot of the stairs.

"Let me see that," said Menucha, taking the tube from Yocheved. "Zinc for diaper rash and—"

"And sunscreen," said Yocheved indignantly. "Tatti gave it to me once to use."

Shira rolled her eyes. "That's because he was desperate," said Menucha, "and we didn't have anything else in the house."

"Well," said Yocheved, "we don't have anything else now either. Who's going to sing around with me?"

"A *round* you mean," said Shira. "Does this look like what I think it does?"

She reached up a tentative finger and wiped it across the bridge of her nose. Her finger was instantly coated with a white, greasy substance that did not wipe off easily despite her vigorous rubbing.

"I think we'll stop for that sunscreen after all," said Shira, "once we're in the car. What time does Mazon open on Sundays? We can get the sunscreen there and pick up some nosh, too."

"I don't know," said Simcha with a shrug.

"They always put an ad in the Nu Hempstead News," said Menucha. "We can find the time there. It's supposed to come in the mail on Fridays, but we didn't get it yet so it probably came on Shabbos."

"I want to sing around!" Yocheved insisted.

"The mail!" said Shira. "I forgot about the mail. It's still out there. I'll get it now. Okay, Yocheved, Menucha will start the song, and you join in when I say now."

"I'm out of here," said Simcha. "I'll get the drink boxes in the freezer, and then I'm plugging my ears."

"*Row, Row, Row Your*—" Menucha started lustily as Shira turned the handle to get the mail from the box next to the front door. "*Bo*—"

Menucha's song ground to an instant halt as Shira opened the door. There, hand suspended, stood Mrs. Rosenman ready to ring the bell, but too shocked to do so as her ears were accosted by Menucha's overly hearty tune.

Acutely embarrassed at how she looked, Shira winced as Mrs. Rosenman's eyes traveled in stunned disbelief from Menucha to Shira's turbaned head gear, painted face, down to the water-stained shoulders of her shirt, finally resting longest on Shira's bare toes. The mess of still-to-be-loaded trip items in the hall, in clear view beyond the open door, didn't help matters either. Mortified, Shira thought about closing the door and setting the deadbolt as she had the night before, but she realized it wasn't going to work today.

"You're here for the dish?" Shira said weakly as a curious Yocheved came and peered under Shira's elbow at Mrs. Rosenman. "I'm so sorry! I forgot all about it."

"Actually, I came to let you know I won't be needing it," said Mrs. Rosenman roughly. "Maybe I should send over the phone number of that gal I was about to hire to lend you a hand in cleaning up, though you'll have to keep an eye on her. I won't be needing her as there won't be any party."

"Thanks," said Shira, recovering rapidly, "but we won't be needing anyone to help clean either. We're on our way out."

"Dressed like that?" Mrs. Rosenman said acidly as she turned heel to go.

"What happened to the birthday party?" Yocheved called after her.

"Shush," said Menucha as Mrs. Rosenman stumped off towards home without answering. "You know her children have never come to her."

"But she said," Yocheved said.

"That's so sad," said Shira, thoughtfully. "I still think we have to do something about her. Anyway, Menucha, here's the mail, and here's the paper. Let's get moving. Please put all the stuff in the car while I go brush my hair and wash my face."

Shira turned and climbed the stairs.

"Look who gets stuck with all the work," said Menucha, shaking her head.

"Oh, come on," said Simcha. "At least she's taking us on this trip."

"Yeah," said Menucha, "but I wonder why she's really doing it."

"To have fun," suggested Simcha. "That's all she seems to be interested in since she got here. She's always baking with Yocheved, playing games with us and taking us to parks and stuff."

"I just wonder what the *real* reason is," said Menucha, as she bent to take out a load of goods to the car.

THIRTY-TWO

Mrs. Lelchook sat inside her black Lexus with her fingers drumming impatiently on the padded steering wheel, unconsciously avoiding the plethora of buttons that adorned the inner workings of the steering wheel. In her other hand, she clutched the tiny cell phone. Where was Shira? She had been calling repeatedly but all she got was the answering machine. It was Sunday, a perfect day for her to stop by, visit with the kids and have another look around the place. Shira might not encourage her presence, but the kids seemed to eat it up. At least the little girl seemed more than receptive to the idea of having a bubby, and bubby or not, Mrs. Lelchook knew it would be to her advantage to work her way into that little girl's heart, as well as to make inroads with the older ones.

They might be suspicious of Mrs. Lelchook's masquerade as a bubby, but that wasn't going to stop her. She had her own agenda to carry out and if making friends with the three Eisenberg children furthered her goals, she was all for doing just that.

THIRTY-THREE

Sunday morning, July 11

"Shira said we should wait in the car," said Yocheved in consternation as Menucha got out of the front seat and stood outside the car.

"I'm just going inside to see what's taking her so long," said Menucha. "We've been waiting for long enough."

The front door was still wide open and Menucha went in, silent in her Keds. She drew to a stop in the front hall as she heard Shira's voice.

"I know you need the plans," Shira was saying.

She must be talking on the phone, Menucha realized.

"I've looked everywhere, the office, the den, the kitchen. If you don't think I did a good enough job looking, you're welcome to come yourself. We'll be gone all day. Shall I leave you the key under the mat? Yeah, I know, you don't need the key."

What kind of a crook was she talking to? Menucha wondered, as her eye wandered to the two-inch long, heavy deadbolt that she had always thought kept their home secure.

"I understand you'll be out all day, too," Shira went on. "Look, I really have to go. The kids are waiting. I know the designs for the new line are important. I of all people can understand that. Yes, I'll keep looking. You found nothing in his office at work? Okay, I'll look all over again—but this is the last time, really."

Why were the designs so important? Menucha tiptoed closer to her father's office where Shira was talking. Probably because with a new line, if her father's competitors could beat him to the stores, they would earn the credit due her father for creating a new trend, and everyone would want their jewelry instead of her father's. More and more, Menucha was beginning to understand exactly how important it was for her to save her father's competitors from discovering where he had hidden his latest designs.

It didn't take much of an epiphany for Menucha to realize what the next best thing to convincing her father would be. She backed up slowly into the hall she had just come from and headed straight for the little bench beside the front door. Shira's purse was sitting on the bench. The side pocket was for a cell phone, and as Menucha had suspected, her father's cell phone was nestled right inside the pocket. She lifted the Velcro fastener and removed the phone. She took it into the kitchen and, after a quick glance at the list of telephone numbers on the bulletin board, she started to dial. The number was busy, but Menucha tried the second line, since her father had written down both numbers on the list.

"Hi, Mrs. Walberg," she said, after reaching behind her to close the door to the kitchen. "It's me, Menucha. ... Yeah, we're on our way out real soon. When do you think you'll be leaving? ... I'm glad you didn't leave yet, because since you're leaving soon, too, I figured you could use an extra hand with the kids. ... Yeah, I'll just walk over and help you load up the van and the kids. ... No, Shira won't care. Why should she? ... Okay. I'll be over after Shira leaves with everyone else, say in about an hour."

With a quick glance over her shoulder, Menucha was down the hall and out the front door before Shira had even finished her own conversation.

"Listen, guys," she said to her waiting siblings in the car. "I'm going over to help the Walbergs."

"I want to come!" said Yocheved.

"Not this time," said Menucha hastily. "Just tell Shira for me, and tell her I took the cell phone, too, but don't tell her until you're about halfway to White Lake. I don't want her to come and get it from me."

"Tell her yourself," said a sulking Simcha who was tired of sitting in the hot car waiting to leave.

"I can't!" said Menucha desperately. "Shira's going to come out of the front door any minute now. Just tell her that Mrs. Walberg needed my help. I'll meet you up at the lake." Menucha turned and ran around to the back of the house.

"If she's going to the Walbergs," Yocheved said, turning to her brother, "then how come she just went back to the house?"

"How am I supposed to know?" asked Simcha, who had been thinking the same thing.

"Ready to go?" Shira asked as she came out of the house and slipped into the driver's seat. "Wait! Where's Menucha?"

"She went to help the Walbergs," Yocheved said. "I guess they'll drive her there in their car."

"When did Mrs. Walberg arrange all that?" asked a mystified Shira.

"Just a minute ago," said Yocheved. "Can we go now? I can't wait to go swimming. It's so hot already."

"It sure is," said Shira, starting the car so that the air conditioning could go on full blast. "I'm glad Mr. Walberg gave us the key. I guess he knew we would beat him up there, even with that stop we have to make at Mazon."

"*Row, row, row your boat,*" Yocheved began to sing cheerfully as they backed out of the driveway.

"Am I going to have to listen to you sing the whole way?" groaned Simcha.

"Not if you sing with me," Yocheved sang right on tune.

None of the three in the car noticed the twitch of the curtains in the house behind them or the face in the window of the house next door.

THIRTY-FOUR

Sunday morning, July 11

The shadchan picked up the phone and dialed, knowing full well that being pushy was frequently the only way to press people into taking that often scary first step. She had discovered over the years that all people really needed was a little encouragement and a lot of nagging. This case was really taking the cake, though. She had already left more messages then she could count, but how could she press her case if her calls were never returned?

"Give it one last shot," she cajoled herself. "You know when you've got a good thing going."

She knew it so well that she called back no less than five times, but each time it was only the answering machine and she had already left enough messages.

"At this point he can just call me," she muttered to herself, slamming down the phone after her fifth try. "If he ever gets my messages, that is."

Thinking dark thoughts about the woman who had taken her previous calls was enough to ruin the rest of her day, despite the perfect weather. Deep down, she knew she wasn't going to give up even if he was not the one to call her back. He had to come home sometime, and wearing the feather in her cap of having made a shidduch for none other than Binyamin Eisenberg, the handsome and wealthy entrepreneur, was something her whole being craved, no matter how many times she had to chase him down. It was going to be worth it! She could feel it in her bones.

THIRTY-FIVE

Sunday morning, July 11

It was time for Menucha to take matters into her own hands. With Shira safely out of the way, she was free to do what was needed to save her father's business. If Shira was really a spy, and Menucha really wanted people to believe her, what she needed most was proof. She had one hour to find that proof, and she was ready.

She ran back to her house. As soon as she opened the front door, she could hear the phone ringing. She quickly decided to ignore it. It continued ringing, five times in a row, without a single message being left on the answering machine in between each call. Menucha pounded up the stairs towards the small guest room, now Shira's room, only stopping for a split second to check the driveway through the window at the landing to make sure that they hadn't turned around for some forgotten item or other. The driveway was empty, so Menucha continued up the stairs and down the hall. Pushing open Shira's door, Menucha paused guiltily in the doorway as the faint scent of Shira's perfume wafted over her, but her pause was only for a split second. She had to do this. After all, she was fighting for her father's business.

A quick survey of the room gave Menucha no hint of where to start. The light wooden dresser top was covered with odds and ends that Shira had tossed about in her hurry to get out to the lake this morning. Various articles of clothing spilled out of the drawers that for the most part were still wide open. The matching night table beside the bed was decorated with a wide variety of make-up and lotions. Rising up from among the numerous bottles and containers was Shira's digital clock with windchimes. Yocheved had already excitedly described to Menucha how setting the alarm caused the small fan inside the clock to blow. This in turn set the windchimes gently tinkling, which was certainly a better way to wake up, to Menucha's mind at least, and obviously Shira's as well, than the startling noise that most alarm clocks blasted.

Menucha decided her best bet would be to start with the roll-top desk, which was surprisingly neat and painstakingly arranged, unlike the rest of the room, except for the wrinkle-free flowered summer quilt that covered the bed and hung down perfectly on all four sides.

Menucha sifted through a pile of papers in the top desk drawer, but discovered nothing of interest. She made her first find in the middle drawer. In Shira's handwriting was the code to her father's safe. She recognized it instantly because her father had told her that he had used her birth date to set and remember it by. It was even written on stationary that read: *From the desk of: Shira Baum* on the top.

After searching the desk, closet and night table, Menucha turned towards the larger dresser, with a hutch that surrounded a mirror, for her final attempt. She had forty-five minutes left before she had to leave to the Walbergs, and she knew she needed more proof than the one piece of paper clutched in her hand.

Hand on the drawer, she paused as she heard the sound of a car pulling into the driveway. She ran to the window and looked outside just in time to see the stately, elegant figure of "Bubby" get out of the car. What was *she* doing here?

The sound of Mrs. Lelchook's high heels on the porch sent Menucha into a panic. Was this the unknown individual that Shira had been talking to before, the one who didn't need the key for some reason? She must have come to search the house as well. Menucha looked around the room for a moment in a panic. Then she dove under Shira's bed and rolled as far under it as she could go, which was up against the back wall. Her trembling fingers brushed against what she thought was the side of the wall but she soon realized that it wasn't the wall after all. It was something else. She would have to take a look at it later, when she knew it was safe.

Menucha wriggled uncomfortably under the bed, reaching under her left side to remove whatever it was she lying on top of. The feel of the object sent needles of excitement racing through Menucha. She recognized the soft velvety covering and feel of a snap-lid jewelry box. If Shira was such a neat person, then why would she keep it here under her bed where not even a dustball dared to reside? Obviously the jewelry box and other item were here for a reason: to keep them safe from the prying eyes of the Eisenberg children.

"Hello!" called Mrs. Lelchook, her voice carrying up from outside to the open window of Shira's bedroom. "Anybody home?"

Even more proof, Menucha thought, that this woman was not Shira's mother. What daughter wouldn't tell her mother about a trip to White Lake that she was going to take?

"Shira?" Mrs. Lelchook tried again, rattling the doorknob and knocking loudly. "Children? Yocheved? Menucha? Simcha? I thought I'd pop by for a visit. Anybody home?"

Menucha heaved a sigh of relief when she heard the car door slam and the purring of the engine as the car backed out of the driveway. So, this wasn't the person Shira had been talking to after all. There were even more people involved in this spying network than Menucha had originally imagined. And this other person had a key!

Crawling out from under the bed, Menucha brought out both of her prizes. The first made her gasp in shock. It was a red velvet jewelry box. Nestled inside was a stunning set of what could only be her father's finest signature series of jewelry. Menucha knew this because she pored over all of her father's jewelry catalogues before they were ever sent out to his distributors. This bracelet and necklace set, with alternating pearl and diamond flowers, Menucha was sure she had seen in her father's latest catalogue, and the jewelry was not even scheduled to hit the market until the fall.

At this point, Menucha decided she had enough evidence to call her father. She had put his cell phone into the deep pocket of her jean skirt. Her father's cell phone was equipped with a camera, a perk that he had gotten when he had signed up for his calling plan. The camera was perfect for what Menucha needed it for, and luckily her father had shown her how to take pictures and save them on the computer or send them to his e-mail address. She aimed the cell phone and clicked. Now she had the proof she needed!

After taking several shots of both the jewelry set and Shira's stationary with the combination code written on it, Menucha turned her attention to the second thing she had discovered under the bed. It was a zippered folder she had retrieved from against the wall. One look at the sheaf of papers in her hand and Menucha was positive that she now had more than enough proof to use against her mysterious babysitter. What was her father's employee doing with jewelry designs? Though they were not the designs of her father's upcoming line, still these designs were definitely her father's.

Several minutes and multiple pictures later, Menucha had the computer switched on in her father's office and was downloading all of the images she had just taken. She put a disk into the drive and clicked on the save command. The computer whirred softly and copied most of the pictures, but when she was almost at the end, it stopped. The number of pictures she was trying to save was just too large for one disk. This had happened before and Menucha knew just what to do. She reached up onto the shelf above the computer, took down an unused zip disk, and inserted it into the zip drive. This time, her save went smoothly, and all of the pictures were copied. Menucha turned off the computer and replaced her father's cell phone in its cradle. Disk in hand, she was now more than ready to go.

THIRTY-SIX

"It was so thoughtful of you to come help us out," said Ephraim Walberg as Menucha helped him load the gold minivan for the trip.

The Walbergs had a lot more to bring, since they would be staying in White Lake for the week, while Shira and the Eisenbergs were only going for the day.

"It was nothing," said Menucha, smiling broadly in anticipation of the captive audience she would have in the van on the drive up.

Ephraim was glad to see that Menucha was so excited about the trip. He ran his fingers through his short, brown beard as he mentally calculated everything they needed to bring. He double-checked that his mountain bike was safely locked onto the bike rack on the van's roof before jogging back to the house for a few last minute items.

"All set?" Rivky Walberg asked, her yellow cotton snood slightly askew as she came out of the house, blue eyes sparkling with excitement despite being loaded down with baby, diaper bag and the three- and four-year-old boys who were clinging to either side of her long, khaki skirt.

"Just about," Mr. Walberg said, slamming the back of the van closed. "All aboard."

"Who has to go to the bathroom?" Rivky asked.

Refael and Aryeh both shook their heads in the negative vehemently.

"So, let's go," Ephraim said.

The two boys climbed into their respective car and booster seats while Mrs. Walberg buckled the baby into his car seat. Menucha found herself all the way in the back, since the three car seats took up the whole second seat of the minivan. With Mr. and Mrs. Walberg in the front, an already cranky baby in the middle with his two brothers arguing over every last thing, it didn't look like it was going to be as easy as she had originally hoped to hold the Walbergs as her captive audience as she explained the Shira situation to them.

"I wanna piece of gum," Aryeh whined.

"I just gave you one!" Rivky said, turning around to face the boys.

"I swallowed it," said Aryeh.

"If you swallow the next piece," said Mrs. Walberg, passing her son another piece, "you aren't going to get anymore."

"Tell him to stop chewing so loud," Refael whined as they turned onto the Palisades Parkway.

"Refael is looking at me," Aryeh cried. "Tell him to stop."

All the while the baby fretted, tugging at his car seat buckles and trying to arch his back. He would suck his two middle fingers and drowse for a few seconds of blessed silence only to be jolted back awake by his brother's newest arguments.

Menucha leaned back in her seat seething. It was only about an hour's drive to get to White Lake, but unless she started whining and fretting, too, it didn't look like she was going to get the Walbergs' attention.

"I have to go to the bathroom," Refael announced fifteen minutes into the drive.

"I asked you if you had to go before we left the house," Rivky said in exasperation.

"I didn't have to go then," said Refael.

"Well, we're not stopping now," said his father.

"I have to go to the bathroom, too," said Aryeh, the first time he had been in agreement with his brother about anything since Menucha had arrived to help an hour ago.

"Ephraim," Rivky said, noting her husband's tensed shoulders. "I'm sorry but we're going to have to stop."

"Okay, okay," said Ephraim, turning off at the next exit and pulling up to the pump at the first gas station, which happened to be full service. "I can fill up here anyway, once we're here already."

"Let's go," said Mrs. Walberg, unbuckling the boys.

"I don't have to," said Aryeh, putting his buckle back on.

"What do you mean you don't have to?" said Mr. Walberg. "You just told me two minutes ago—"

"Don't have to," Aryeh repeated stubbornly, clutching the sides of his car seat with no intention of letting go.

"Okay," said Mrs. Walberg, "but we aren't stopping again until we get there."

She marched off with Refael in tow, while Mr. Walberg rolled down his window to speak to the attendant.

"Fill it up with super, please," he said.

Seizing the opportunity, with the baby being asleep at last and no siblings around for any noisy sibling rivalry, Menucha moved from her seat to the floor of the second row of the van, one row closer to her intended target, Mr. Walberg.

"Only another forty-five minutes plus multiple pit stops along the way," said Mr. Walberg genially when he noticed Menucha behind him.

"Mr. Walberg," Menucha said, leaning forward with a sense of urgency. "I really need to speak with you. That's why I came with you today."

"Speak with *me*?" Mr. Walberg said in surprise. "Whatever for?"

"It's about Shira," said Menucha.

"Ah, Shira," said Mr. Walberg, smiling warmly at Menucha. "Isn't she great? I knew you would like her."

"Well..." said Menucha uncomfortably.

"Yeah," said Mr. Walberg, stretching his arms and legs. "Shira's something special, isn't she? Your father made the right decision to leave you kids with her. You really like her, don't you?"

"Not exactly," said Menucha, flushing.

"Not exactly?" said Mr. Walberg in astonishment. "Why on earth not?"

"See, I've tried speak with my father, but he refuses to listen."

"Well, if he refuses to listen," said Mr. Walberg, looking decidedly uncomfortable, "then why should—"

"Mr. Walberg," said Menucha. "This is extremely important for both you and my father. Shira is out to destroy your business. I'm sure of it. She's a spy."

"A spy?" Mr. Walberg sputtered as he distractedly passed his credit card out the window to the attendant.

"Yes," said Menucha. "And I have proof. I took pictures of some terribly suspicious things that I found in Shira's room. You won't believe what I found hidden under her bed and in her desk."

"I won't believe it," Mr. Walberg repeated slowly as he watched the attendant walk slowly into the store to run the card through the machine.

"Right," said Menucha. "We have to do something, since—"

"Did you see that?" Mr. Walberg interrupted. "That guy just used my credit card to clean out his teeth. He expects me to touch it after that?"

"Mr. Walberg," Menucha said. "Were you listening to me? I just said my father won't listen to me. I took pictures of—"

"Now he's coming back out," Mr. Walberg moaned, "and he just used his pen to clean out his ear. There is no way I'm touching that pen now. Who knows what kind of germs that guy has."

"Here," said Menucha. "There's a pen here on the floor so you won't have to use his." Menucha picked up a blue pen from the minivan floor and gave it to Mr. Walberg. "Anyway, like I was saying, I took pictures of everything I found in Shira's room with my father's cell phone camera so I would have proof."

She held out the zip disk for Mr. Walberg to take, just as the gas station attendant returned with his receipt and a pen for him to sign.

"No, thanks," Mr. Walberg said to the attendant. "I have my own pen."

He signed the credit receipt with the pen Menucha gave him and gingerly took back his credit card, which he then fastidiously wiped off with the antiseptic wipes his wife kept in the van for cleaning the children.

"Don't you want to take it?" Menucha asked after Mr. Walberg had replaced his wallet.

"No, he used that pen to clean out his ear. Didn't you see that?"

"Not the pen, the zip disk I copied for you. Here. Please take it."

But Mr. Walberg was distracted. He looked around wildly for a moment, his eyes resting nervously on the zip disk for a split second before lighting on the bathroom door which his wife and son had disappeared through moments before.

"Aryeh," Mr. Walberg said, his voice tight with tension. "You really do have to go to the bathroom. I can tell."

"No, I do—"

"You are coming to the bathroom, *now*," Mr. Walberg said, reaching out to unbuckle his son and opening the door beside him. "Let's go."

"But, Mr. Walberg," Menucha said in shock. "I just wanted to tell you—"

"Aryeh is having something of an emergency," Mr. Walberg said as he unbuckled his son.

"I don't haffta—" Aryeh protested, trying to hold his car seat buckle in the lock position, but he was no match for his determined father.

"We'll be right back," Mr. Walberg said, hefting his still struggling three-year-old into his arms.

There was nothing Menucha could do but wait. She climbed back into her seat, but not after first leaving the zip disk on the driver's seat for Mr. Walberg to see when he returned.

"What's this?" Mrs. Walberg asked as she got back with Rafael before her husband had returned.

"It's for Mr. Walberg to look at when he has a chance," said Menucha.

"Okay," said Mrs. Walberg. "It won't be until sometime Monday though. We don't have a computer in the lake house. I guess you lucked out though. The kids and I are going to be there for the week, but Ephraim is going to be commuting starting tomorrow morning so he can hold down the fort at work with your father gone."

"That's okay if he can't look at it right away," said Menucha, still wondering what to make of Mr. Walberg's strange reaction. "Just tell him to call me once he's had a chance to look it over, or on second thought, I'll speak to him on Monday sometime at work then."

"Fine," said Mrs. Walberg, buckling her seatbelt as her husband returned to the car.

THIRTY - SEVEN

Sunday afternoon, July 11

"I wonder what can be taking them so long," said Shira, as she sat on the dock, her feet dangling in the waters of the lake.

It was a perfect day to spend by the lake. The morning mist had burned off completely, leaving the sun shining brightly as the waves lapped gently against the shore. The wooden dock, similar to the docks all along the shore line, reached far enough out in the lake to be deep enough for the motor boat to be tied up alongside it. A small, sandy beach with a child-size plastic slide kept Refael and Aryeh busy digging, sliding and splashing in the shallow water, though both of them still wore brightly colored life preservers.

"They'll get here soon enough," said Simcha, casting his fishing line out into the lake.

"Not near us next time, okay?" Shira cautioned after the fishing line whizzed too close to her head for comfort.

"There aren't any fish here anyway," said Simcha. "I'm going out in the canoe. Is that okay?" he asked Mrs. Walberg, who was watching her boys.

"Please, be my guest," Mrs. Walberg smiled.

"I'm coming, too," said Yocheved, jumping down to the spit of sand beside the dock and pushing the canoe off the beach so that its head was afloat in the lake.

"Not too far," cautioned Simcha. "You don't want it to float away before I get there."

"Wait for me," said Shira.

"You're coming, too?" asked Simcha.

"Someone has to look after Yocheved," said Shira, reaching under the canoe seat for a life jacket and buckling it on after passing one to Yocheved and another to Simcha.

"Let's go," said Yocheved jumping up and down.

"You sit in the middle," Simcha ordered his sister.

"I'll sit in the back," Shira volunteered, climbing in gingerly and sitting down.

"Uh, Shira?" said Simcha.

"What is it?" Shira asked. "Did you want to sit here, and I'll sit in the front?"

"No, you can sit there," said Simcha.

"Good," said Shira, reassured. "I've never gone in one of these things before," she explained, smiling.

"That's obvious," said Simcha, "because I can't push the boat off with you in there. You're too heavy when we're still partway on the beach. You're going to have to climb in once we're in the water."

"But I'll get all wet," Shira protested.

"I thought that was why we came to the lake," said Simcha.

"Right," said Shira. "That does make sense. No problem. I'll get out and you can get in, and I'll get in after I see how you do it."

"If you insist," said Simcha, wading out a little ways and climbing into the front of the canoe.

"Okay," said Shira. "All aboard."

She followed the boat into slightly deeper water, wading in after it, her long, denim skirt getting soaked.

"Now what?" she asked nervously once the boat was afloat and she was still standing beside it knee deep in water. "I don't think I quite caught how you did that."

"You climb in," said Simcha.

Shira moved to comply.

"But just make sure to keep yourself down low and center yourself before—"

"Yowwww!" screamed Yocheved as Shira climbed in and accidentally tipped the boat too much. Suddenly Simcha, Yocheved and Shira were in the water as the boat turned over.

"Help! Help!" screamed Yocheved as she floundered beside the capsized boat.

"I'm coming!" Shira cried, splashing to her side.

"Why don't you just try to stand up," said Simcha in disgust as he attempted to turn the boat over, only to have it fill with water during the course of the flip.

"I can stand!" screamed Yocheved in delight. "So what do I need this for?"

She pointed to her orange life vest.

"The idea is to go out much farther than this," said Simcha, "to where you *can't* stand, but first we have to get the boat turned over so we can try again."

A dripping Shira had the good grace to look guilty as she waded over, her denim skirt sloshing loudly with each step to Simcha to help him with the boat.

"Lift the boat while it's still upside down," Simcha instructed. Then turn it over so it doesn't fill with water. Good. Now one, two, three, lift."

Straining under the weight of the metal boat, the pair managed to lift and turn it so that the boat didn't take in water as it flipped.

"Good job!" said Simcha, grinning at the sopping Shira. "I think we'll make a sailor of you yet, as long as we keep you in the shallow water."

"I'm not so sure about that," said Shira, picking a piece of lake grass from her dripping, sandy brown hair and watching as both Yocheved and Simcha climbed back into the boat gracefully, barely rocking the sides as they entered. Her entrance was not quite so smooth, but at least this time the boat stayed afloat and Simcha was able to begin paddling out to the center of the lake.

"Hey!" called a voice from shore.

The threesome looked up to see the distant figure of Ephraim Walberg waving cheerfully. Menucha was at his side.

"Glad you made it," Shira called, cupping her hands and standing up to be heard.

"No, Shira!" Simcha called, just as the boat turned over and all three fell into the water once again.

"Now I see why I need this," said Yocheved, patting her life vest cheerfully as she bobbed in the water beside the overturned boat. "I never knew canoeing was so much fun. Can we go on this ride again, Shira?"

"*You* can," muttered Shira impatiently, wondering how they were going to turn the boat back over when she couldn't touch bottom, "but this is one ride I guess I was not meant for. Once we get this turned back over, I'm heading back for shore!"

THIRTY-EIGHT

Sunday afternoon, July 11

"1442 Sobey Road," the radio squawked in Officer Scott's ear.

"You've got to be kidding," Officer Scott moaned as he reached for the handset to respond as the closest officer in the area. "Now what's she got?"

"Vandals," was the impersonal reply on the radio. "The woman claims hoodlums have been knocking over her garbage cans on a nightly basis."

"—and I tell you, I'm just fed up with it," Mrs. Rosenman said several minutes later as she stood outside her front door, tapping one scruffy, slipper-clad toe as Officer Scott looked down at the garbage scattered all over her driveway from the overturned can.

"I can understand that," he said, stepping gingerly around the mess.

"First my flowers and now this," Mrs. Rosenman continued complaining. "I've had quite enough of dealing with the criminal element of this town."

"Criminal element," Officer Scott sputtered, thinking of the city he had recently been transferred from and what was considered criminal there—certainly not spilled garbage. "Lady, if you only knew what 'criminal element' really meant!"

"Listen, Officer," Mrs. Rosenman grumped, "if you had to put up with this day after day, I don't think you'd like it any better than me."

"No, I don't suppose so," said Officer Scott, studying a muddy print on the side of the beige Rubbermaid garbage can.

"Any fingerprints or anything you can use to go after those vandals?" Mrs. Rosenman asked hopefully.

"Maybe," Officer Scott said. "I can tell you this much, though. Your vandals are masked."

"Amazing," said Mrs. Rosenman. "You can tell all that just from looking? How do you do that?"

"Simple," said Officer Scott, pointing to the print.

Mrs. Rosenman bent over to peer more closely at the muddy shape on the side of her can.

"That's a hand print," she said, straightening with difficulty. "They must start awfully young around here, I can't imagine any teenager having a handprint that size."

"It's not a teenager, Ma'am," said Officer Scott, rolling his eyes.

"Then what are you trying to tell me," Mrs. Rosenman snapped, "that there are two-year-old bandits running around here?"

"No," said Officer Scott, "I'm trying to tell you that your masked vandal is a raccoon."

"You're a city boy, aren't you?" was the scornful reply. "What do you know about coon prints? This is a hand print, clear as day. See? One, two, three, four, five fingers. This is not an animal paw."

"Oh, I give up," said Officer Scott as he stalked off toward his car, "Look, I suggest you just lock the lids of the can next time by pulling up the handles over the lid like they're designed to be."

"What is that going to do?" Mrs. Rosenman sputtered.

"Just answer me this," Officer Scott said, as he reached his car after sauntering carefully around moldy orange rinds, eggshells and other bits of debris. "Do you lock the handles over the can or do you just put on the lids?"

"Well, I *never*," said Mrs. Rosenman. "I didn't think I called you here today to interrogate me!"

"Just answer my question," Officer Scott pressed.

"Sometimes I do, and sometimes I don't," Mrs. Rosenman sniffed. "Sometimes I just can't be bothered, like if the garbage sticks out just a weentsy little bit, it's too hard to lock the handles over the top, since the top doesn't fit."

"Like yesterday?" Officer Scott asked.

"Like yesterday," Mrs. Rosenman acquiesced.

"Well then take my advice," Officer Scott said, climbing into his jeep and leaning out of his open window. "Lock the handles over your lids, and you won't have this kind of trouble again."

He was trying to decide whether or not to be grateful for the series of lectures he had sat through with a renowned tracker. It had helped him to recognize deer prints in Mrs. Rosenman's garden before, and it helped him now to realize that what he was looking at on the side of the garbage can was a clear print from a raccoon paw, but it hadn't earned him much respect, at least not in Mrs. Rosenman's book.

"As if I called him here to give me advice," Mrs. Rosenman muttered as she stalked back inside and slammed her front door.

She was not looking forward to cleaning up her driveway, any more than Officer Scott was looking forward to another day of pretty much the same small town crime, if you could even call his last call a crime scene. Maybe he should reconsider going back to the city. Deer and raccoons were just *not* the kind of criminals he had planned to pursue when he had gone to the police academy years ago.

THIRTY-NINE

"Why don't we get the barbecue going?" Rivky suggested after an afternoon of fishing, boating and building sandcastles on the tiny spit of sand next to the water. "Ephraim, do you want to start the grill?"

"I have an even better idea," said Ephraim, passing his fishing pole to Refael.

"What?" asked Refael.

"Wait and see," said Ephraim. "Where are the hot dogs, Rivky?"

"I'll get them for you," said Menucha eagerly, looking up from the sandcastle she was helping Aryeh build.

"Good idea," said Rivky, "since you put the stuff away in the house for me while I was changing the kids."

"Okay, let's go," said Menucha, getting up and dusting the sand off of her blue cotton skirt.

"Wait!" said Ephraim, looking decidedly nervous. "I think Refael has a nibble."

"I do?" said the surprised boy.

"Quick!" said Ephraim, grabbing a hold of the limp rod still in his son's hands. "We don't want it to get away."

"I don't see anything," said Rivky, looking at the fishing line dangling loosely in the water.

"Me neither," said Simcha, watching for any telltale signs that a fish was on Refael's line.

"Are you sure there's something there?" Rivky asked, still eyeing the limp fishing line with disbelief.

"Don't worry about it," said Ephraim, still holding tight to the rod, which his son gripped fiercely alongside him. "If it's there, we won't let it get away. Oh, and Menucha?"

"Yes?" she asked.

"How about you go into the house and just lay out everything I'll need on the table," Ephraim suggested. "I'll be up in a little bit to start things."

"No problem," said Menucha, giving the still limp fishing pole a suspicious glance.

Was Mr. Walberg avoiding her?

Her suspicions were confirmed over and over as she recalled how time after time when she had tried to maneuver herself into a position to talk to Mr. Walberg privately, he had offered one excuse after another. He always managed to escape Menucha's attempts to speak with him. She had made numerous tries whenever they were out of earshot of the rest of the crowd, and most especially out of the earshot of Shira.

"Can I just say—" she tried when Mr. Walberg went up to start the barbecue, minus whatever fish had allegedly been on Refael's line that seemed to have gotten away.

"Sorry, gotta run," Ephraim said, rushing past her.

"I'll help," Menucha offered.

"No, no, no," said Mr. Walberg. "My wife needs help keeping an eye on the boys."

"But Shira can help her with that," Menucha said.

"No," said Ephraim. "Shira has her hands full with Yocheved."

"Uh, right," said Menucha, glancing over at Yocheved, who had fallen asleep on a sandy blanket under the huge umbrella Shira had erected over her.

Lunch was a do-it-yourself deal. Ephraim had made a fire in the pit nearby instead of starting up the gas grill. Surrounded by a ring of stones, it was the perfect campfire and all the kids looked throughout the backyard, under the trees and bushes, to find a stick to roast the hot dogs.

"I'll take care of that," said Simcha, whipping out a pocket-knife and sharpening the end of Menucha's stick for her when she returned with her find.

"Me, too!" cried the two Walberg boys, holding out the flimsy twigs they had located for sharpening.

"You can use mine first," Menucha offered when Simcha appeared to be at a loss for words over how to sharpen such slender branches. "It's bigger."

Anything bigger was more attractive to Refael and Aryeh.

They quickly dropped their twigs and reached for Menucha's stick.

"I got it first!" Aryeh said fiercely.

"No, me!" said Rafael.

"Come here, Aryeh," Simcha beckoned. "Let's go find an even bigger stick."

"Let's use this one," Menucha told Refael, who was all ready to go dashing off with Simcha in search of a bigger and thus better stick for roasting his hot dog. "We'll go first."

It didn't take Simcha long to return with a new stick for Aryeh. Soon both boys, under the watchful eye of their mother, were roasting their hot dogs in the snapping flames.

"Uh, oh," said Aryeh as his hot dog slid into the hottest part of the fire.

"Here," said Rivky, getting out another hot dog from the package on the nearby picnic table, "try again."

Aryeh tried to slide the new hot dog onto the stick, but to no avail.

"The point of the stick burned off," Simcha observed as he came forward to try to rescue the errant hot dog that had fallen into the flames.

"Mine, too," said Yocheved, as her hot dog slid into the flames.

"So much for self-service," muttered Ephraim, as his plans for his kids and guests to have an outdoor camping experience went up in smoke. "Let me see if I can find something in the house that we can use instead of sticks." Ephraim turned and walked back towards the flight of stairs that led up to the small porch and the door to the living room of the beach house. "I'm going to the house. I have an idea."

"I know what we can use," said Menucha.

She followed Ephraim up to the house, though he was too far ahead for her to catch up to.

Ephraim had disappeared into the kitchen before Menucha even got inside, but Menucha wasn't going into the kitchen. She stopped at the front hall closet to remove a few wire hangers.

"How about these?" she asked, startling Ephraim in the kitchen.

"I guess we'll just have to forget about this campfire business," said Ephraim hastily as soon as he saw Menucha. "I'll go out and tell them."

"But we can use these," said Menucha again, as Ephraim fled out of the seldom-used kitchen door to go the long way around back to the campfire in the backyard.

What was he so nervous about? Why was he so afraid to listen to anything Menucha might have to say? This whole thing was too ridiculous for words, unless, unless, Ephraim and Shira—but no, that was even more ridiculous. Menucha shook the thought from her mind. Ephraim couldn't be in cahoots with Shira, or could he? Why was Ephraim avoiding her? It was all too strange. Right now, though, she had to go rescue the barbecue.

Menucha reappeared from inside the beach house dangling her handful of wire hangers.

"What are those for?" asked Shira.

"We're going to cook hangers?" asked a puzzled Yocheved.

"Brilliant idea, Menucha!" said Simcha, stepping forward to help.

Rivky looked up. "Menucha, that's so smart!"

Simcha and Menucha worked quickly to unwind the twisted

neck of the hangers and fashion the dangling wire into long skewers, Simcha curved his up at the ends so that the hot dogs wouldn't fall off, and Menucha quickly followed suit.

"Aren't they going to burn the boys' fingers?" asked Rivky doubtfully.

"Metal does transmit heat," Shira agreed.

But the distance from the fire to the fingers of the children who were roasting was long enough that hot wires were not a problem. Within minutes there were enough roasted hot dogs to go around.

The remainder of the day was spent pretty much the same, fishing, boating, enjoying the water. Menucha tried to enjoy herself despite her frustrations. Filling in Simcha on all that had happened took up some of her time, and planning their next move took up the rest of it. She hoped her time there had not been in vain when it came to helping to save her father's business, despite the strange reaction of his partner and supposedly close friend.

"He'll change his tune real fast," Simcha comforted Menucha in a whisper as they rode back later that evening from White Lake. "He'll take you more seriously when he sees the files you have on that zip disk."

"I sure hope so," said a troubled Menucha, "because if he doesn't, what are we going to do next?"

FORTY

"Who's she talking to?" Menucha mouthed, coming down for breakfast the next morning and finding her brother already seated at the kitchen table dining on corn flakes liberally sprinkled with chocolate milk powder.

They had gotten home late from White Lake and were all a little groggy.

Shira was pacing the kitchen, clearly nervous as she walked around talking on the cordless phone.

Simcha merely put his fingers to his lips and leaned forward to hear better.

"We've been having a problem with ants here," Shira was saying as she cleared her throat in embarrassment, as if admitting

168

to the ants cast a shadow of doubt on her housekeeping skills.

"Ants. Yes, that's right," said Shira. "No, not the relative kind of ants, the crawling kind."

"The Rav?" Menucha mouthed to her brother, who nodded in agreement.

"So, *motzei Shabbos* I ran the dishwasher," Shira continued. "It was full of them. No, not dishes. Well, yes, it was actually a full load, but I meant it was full of ants as well. I was wondering if the dishes are still kosher. The ants are all gone. Right. Yes, thank you for the advice. We are having an exterminator come today. Yes, he'll be here when the kids are in camp. It's the dishes I'm worried about now. How many ants? How should I know? I mean, the whole dishwasher was really crawling with them. It was like the whole place was moving, but I couldn't possibly guess how many. The water temperature? I really don't know. A shower? I'm talking about the dishwasher, not the shower."

Menucha and Simcha exchanged puzzled glances.

"Yes, I understand. No, it's not unbearably hot when I take a shower with just the hot water on. Yes, I see. Thank you. Thank you so much."

Shira hung up smiling and looked over to the pair at the table.

"I don't know if the Rav has ever had a *shailah* quite like that one. He decided that the number of ants was *batul*. He said that since our hot water heater isn't turned up too high and the dishwasher is a *kli shlishi* or, at the very least, *iruy kli sheini*, the dishes are all fine."

"What a relief!" exclaimed Menucha, still thinking about how upset her father would have been if all those nice Shabbos dishes had suddenly become unusable.

"That's for sure," Shira said, heading for the doorway. "Now, let me go check on Yocheved. I thought she was up a while ago. At this rate, she's going to be late for camp."

"I don't care what kind of proof you've got," said Simcha matter-of-factly as soon as Shira was out of earshot, "she's *not* a spy."

"How do you know?" Menucha asked, going to get the granola from the cupboard behind the table.

"Because if she was a spy," Simcha said, "why would she care to ask the Rav a *shailah*? Someone who was a spy wouldn't care less."

"Maybe it's all a show," said Menucha, momentarily stymied but quickly recovering. "She made the call when she was sure we would be around. This way we would trust her even more. It did make her look good, didn't it? That *has* to be it."

"I guess it can't be anything else," said Simcha with a shrug, "not after what you found in her room and everything else. She sure thinks she has us fooled, doesn't she?"

"Well," said Menucha, her eyes narrowing as she glared in the direction of the doorway through which Shira had disappeared, "she's going to be in for a real big surprise, isn't she?"

FORTY-ONE

"Mr. Walberg?" Miss Peters buzzed her boss. "Mr. Eisenberg's kids are here to see you."

"What?" spluttered Ephraim as his eyes darted nervously around his office. "Tell them I'm tied up. I have a meeting. There's no way—"

The knock on his door told him he was too late. The Eisenberg children knew their way around this office. They had been coming here since they were babies. Clearly, they hadn't needed to wait for the secretary to show them in.

"I'm sorry," Ephraim said, wiping his sweating palms on his black cotton pants before turning the knob to face Menucha and Simcha. "I'm afraid I'm a little tied up right now—"

"I just need to know if you opened up the zip disk I gave you,"

Menucha pressed, putting her foot in the door before Ephraim could close it in her face.

"The zip disk," said Ephraim, wetting his lips nervously. "Oh right, that. Actually, I don't think I had the chance—"

"We can wait while you look at it," suggested Simcha, wondering what was up with his father's usually jovial and friendly partner. This was not the same Ephraim the kids had always known. He looked nervous.

"Actually," said Ephraim, "right, um, actually, I already did try to open that disk, and I didn't see anything because it is empty, completely empty."

"Empty?" said Menucha in shock, "but that can't be. I double-checked it myself. It opened up on my computer! At least I thought it did." Menucha shook her head in dismay.

"Well, empty it is," said Ephraim coldly as he got a hold of himself at last. "Now, I don't know what kind of games you kids are playing, but I really don't have time for any of your shenanigans. Your father isn't going to like it either. Like I said, I'm really busy. I've been trying to do the work of two people ever since your father left, which is never easy. Before you go," he looked at the kids firmly, suddenly taking authority, "I just want to say that I think you guys should lay off of Shira. She's an extremely nice person. Give her a chance. Okay?"

"Give Shira a chance," Menucha repeated dumbly as the door closed in their face. "To do what, ruin Tatti even more?"

"I just don't get it," said Simcha as he and Menucha got out of the elevator and walked out of the four-story office building back towards the bus stop. "Ephraim should be just as worried as we are about all this! Even if he doesn't want to believe any of it, you would think he would at least check into it."

"Unless—" said Menucha, stopping short and grabbing her brother's arm.

"Unless what?" asked Simcha, looking up nervously towards the window of Ephraim's office. Was he watching them from up there to make sure they were gone? He had certainly seemed in an awfully big hurry to get them out of there.

"Unless he's in on it, too!" said Menucha with horror at the thought of their father's tried and true friend stabbing him in the back like that.

"This is getting serious!" said Simcha as they walked down the busy main street.

"Yeah," said Menucha, awed at the ramifications of their words, "too serious."

"What are we going to do next?" asked Simcha, sitting down on the bench in the glass enclosed bus shelter.

"We have to try Tatti again," said Menucha. "He *has* to believe us this time. Now we have even more proof."

"Well, we had proof," said Simcha, "but if that zip disk is blank, or is as good as blank because Ephraim has it, then what proof do we have?"

"It's our word against hers," said Menucha gloomily.

"Yeah," said Simcha, "but I'm beginning to wonder what exactly our word is worth around here. We can't get an adult to listen to us!"

FORTY-TWO

Monday afternoon, July 12

"It took you long enough," said the coarse voice.

"I'm sorry," was the sheepish reply. "I forgot all about it, until today."

"Do they know where you are?"

"I just said I was going out for a little while."

"It's better that way," the voice grunted, before setting down the usual plate of orange tea biscuits and lemonade.

"So?" was the eager question. "Did you find something for me?"

"A few of these would do for you," was the appraising reply. "Get the papers and we'll go over it. You'll have the final say. It is for you after all and it's all extremely nice stuff. You certainly can't go wrong, whatever you decide."

"Yeah, I suppose so. Can we look now?"

Two heads, one wrinkled and grey and the other, smaller, with shiny, dark hair, bent over and studied the pages in minute detail.

"Are you sure it's good for me?" the visitor asked at last, looking up from the page they had been mulling over the longest.

"It will do," was the noncommittal reply. "You're extremely lucky, you know, to have a choice like this."

"I know."

"When do they say he'll be home now?"

"No one told me."

"Figures. Well, mark my words. When he gets home there is sure to be trouble."

"You keep saying that."

"Older and wiser."

"Well, I sure hope not. I mean about the trouble. We've tried to do everything right, to stay out of trouble! Oh, I think I have to go."

"Don't forget all these pages."

"I'll come back for them later," was the rushed reply. "I forgot that we're supposed to leave. Do you mind keeping them for me for now?"

"Are you giving me a choice?" was the gruff reply stated to the back of the door, which had already closed due to the hasty exit.

FORTY-THREE

"Where is everyone?" Simcha asked as he and Menucha came in the house.

"Perfect," said Menucha, holding a note that had been left on the otherwise spotless kitchen table. "Shira is out food shopping with Yocheved. Now's our chance, but first let's set up the walkie talkies."

"What are you doing?" Simcha asked as Menucha picked up the set of walkie talkies that was always kept charging on the desk in the kitchen. "Are we going somewhere?"

"I'm setting one of them on lock," said Menucha. "We'll leave it here in the kitchen. That way, when Shira comes home with Yocheved, I'll hear them when they carry the groceries into the kitchen through the garage door, since that's where Shira always comes through."

"And where are we going to be?" asked Simcha, grabbing a handful of oatmeal cookies from the cookie jar on the counter that Shira always made sure to keep well stocked, much to Simcha's gastronomical delight.

"Can you stop thinking about food for a second?" said Menucha, stuffing the second walkie talkie into her skirt pocket, grabbing her brother by the shoulders and propelling him out the door and away from the heady allure of a full cookie jar.

"Wait a second!" Simcha protested, spraying cookie crumbs. "I need a drink."

"You'll just have to wait," said Menucha. "I don't know how long ago they left, so I don't know how much time we have."

"What are we doing in Shira's room?" Simcha asked as Menucha let go of him in the doorway.

"I just want to show you the stuff," grunted Menucha who was on her stomach and peering under the bed.

Simcha studied the heels of his sister's shoes for several minutes, feeling amused, but his sister's expression when she came out from under the bed was not a cause for amusement.

"It's gone!" she said in disbelief. "How could she have known we're on to her? Unless, no, it couldn't be…"

"What?" said Simcha. But he was thinking the same thing. Only one other person knew what had been under the bed.

"Unless Ephraim told her."

"Wow," Simcha said, "this really does prove that Ephraim is in with her. How could he have fooled us all these years?"

"He's a good actor," said Menucha.

"Maybe we've got it all wrong," said Simcha, finding it difficult to accept that they had all been duped for all those years.

"How else could she have known we found the stuff in her room? It's not here now, is it?"

"Wait a second," said Simcha, heading for his room.

He returned moments later with a pocket flashlight that he used to read in bed under his covers at night when it was past his bedtime and the book was just too good to put down.

"I'll look again," said Menucha, "but I really doubt there's anything there. I found it the first time without a flashlight, didn't I?"

"By accident," Simcha pointed out.

"Still," Menucha said, taking the flashlight doubtfully and ducking under the bed once again.

"Nothing," she said shortly thereafter. "Let's try the desk."

But that too was empty. Though the stationary that read *From the desk of: Shira Baum* was still there, the sheet with the combination number was gone. Only the faint impression of what might have been the numbers remained on the otherwise clean top sheet.

"She knows!" Menucha said nervously. "Ephraim must have told her."

"It doesn't matter," said Simcha. "She may have hidden it all away, and Ephraim may have erased it from the zip disk, but you still have it on the computer."

"On the computer?" said Menucha blankly.

"You did save it on the computer before you copied it onto the zip disk, right?" Simcha pressed.

Menucha shook her head in despair.

F O R T Y - F O U R

"Okay," Ephraim said to himself, pacing nervously around the perimeters of his office.

It had been a long afternoon. He had tried to forget the whole unpleasant business with the Eisenberg children, but the bad feelings over the whole event just wouldn't leave him.

"I am not going to let this get to me. This is not a major tragedy—*yet*. They're just kids. They'll get over it. They'll forget. I'm can't let this get to me. It's too important. Those kids don't even know what they're saying. How could they? Why, if they knew the real story, they'd probably fight even harder. Right now they don't really even know what they're up against. This *is* getting completely out of hand, though. I don't know how much longer I can hold out."

Ephraim continued his nervous pacing, his hands locked behind his back. He felt as if all of his carefully laid plans were crumbling down around him. He had been so close, so close to success, and he knew he had to do something before it was too late.

"If they're on to Shira like this," he told himself, "the next person they'll be after is me. I have to cover for myself. I'm not going to take the rap for all this alone. When they confront her, Shira will never be able to stand up for herself. She'll cave in, and it'll be me left holding the bag.

"Maybe this is all my fault. I *did* arrange this whole thing. But this is creating a real emergency." He shook his head in disbelief. "Who would have ever guessed that those kids would react like this?"

The cell phone in his pocket vibrated. Choosing to ignore the incoming call, Ephraim waited until the phone's vibrations stopped. Then he reached for the phone, his hands slippery with sweat. He had to make a call to the one person who would stand up for him under fire despite everything that was going on, despite all the accusations that were being hurled his way. It was time for Binyamin to come home.

FORTY-FIVE

"Doesn't it copy onto the computer when you take it from the camera?" Simcha asked his downcast sister.

"No," said Menucha. "I just opened the pictures from the camera on the computer. Then I tried to save the picture files on diskette, but it didn't fit, so then I had to do it on a zip disk, but I did not save any of the files on the computer. I never thought of that. Why should I have saved it anyway?"

"Now you know why," said Simcha. "Wait! What about the cell phone? Is it still stored in the camera there?"

"No," said a dejected Menucha. "I erased it after I had it on the zip disk. I didn't want to tie up all its memory in case I needed to take some more pictures with it."

"Oh," said a thoughtful Simcha. "Wait a second. I have an idea."

"Whatever," said a listless Menucha as she headed to her room while her brother headed in the opposite direction and pounded down the stairs.

"Menucha! Come quick," Simcha yelled a few minutes later into the walkie talkie in the kitchen, well aware that his sister still had the other handset turned on in her pocket.

"What?" Menucha called from the top of the stairs.

She had tried replying on the walkie talkie but since the other one was still locked on, Simcha hadn't heard her.

"Just come down here to the computer," Simcha said.

At the word "computer," Menucha flew down the stairs, her heart in her mouth. Could it be that Simcha had found something? She had been so sure she hadn't saved a thing on the computer! Still, stranger things had been known to happen when computers were involved.

"How did you do that?" Menucha gasped, staring at the computer screen. Taking up the entire screen was her shot of the jewelry that she had discovered under Shira's bed.

"Simple!" said Simcha, reaching over to the a: drive and popping out a diskette, which he held up to his sister. "You saved this picture on diskette and the one of the file of jewelry designs has a few shots here, too. I presume the rest of the stuff didn't fit, because that's all that's on this diskette."

"It's enough!" said Menucha, elated. "Oh, Simcha thanks so much! Why didn't I think of that? That's the diskette I tried saving everything on the first time around! I didn't realize it wouldn't all fit, and it took me forever to do it all over again on the zip disk."

"But," Simcha said, "it's a good thing it didn't all fit after all. Isn't it? Because now we at least have *some* proof that Ephraim didn't erase."

"Right," said Menucha smiling, her equilibrium restored. "Excellent thinking, little brother."

"Thanks," said a beaming Simcha. "Now what?"

"Now we send these pictures to Ta," said Menucha. "After all, pictures speak louder than words, and we sure haven't gotten very far with our words, have we?"

"How will you send them?" asked Simcha. "Snail mail?"

"No," said Menucha, reaching for the mouse and taking the seat Simcha vacated for her. "E-mail."

"Great idea!" said Simcha. "After that, let's go rollerblading."

"In a minute," said Menucha. "You get on your rollerblades. I'll just attach these files and send it to Ta's address so he can see it the next time he checks his e-mail."

"You ready?" Simcha asked from the driveway when Menucha came out several minutes later and gave him the thumbs up. "I'll get your rollerblades for you."

Simcha skated around to the side of the garage and reached out his hand for the door knob while skating down the short incline towards the door. He was skating faster than he had estimated though. As he put his hand up to slow himself down, his right hand smashed through the glass window pane above the door knob.

"Menucha!" he screamed, holding his arm, now dripping blood all over the sidewalk. "Menucha!" he called again.

Menucha heard his cries and quickly came to him.

"Oh my gosh!" Menucha sobbed when she saw him and the shattered glass at his feet. "What do I do?"

Quickly, she knelt beside her brother who had sunk to the ground and held his arm tightly to stop the blood from oozing out.

"Call Hatzoloh," Simcha gasped, "and stop holding me, you're hurting me."

"I'm not going to let go of you," said Menucha with a catch in her voice. "You're bleeding too much, and I can't very well call Hatzoloh either. I have to hold your arm to stop the bleeding."

She looked hopefully next door toward Mrs. Rosenman's house.

"Why is it that she isn't looking outside now?" she asked bitterly.

But Mrs. Rosenman had been watching, at least once she had heard the tinkle of glass and Simcha's scream. She had spotted the kids and the blood right away, but she had also spotted something else.

"Stop!" Mrs. Rosenman shrieked, running out into the middle of Sobey Road, her pink slippers slapping the pavement as she ran. "Stop!"

"What now?" Officer Scott drawled when he saw his least favorite person of all flagging him down, leaving him no choice but to come to a halt and reluctantly roll down the window.

"The kids!" Mrs. Rosenman wheezed. "It's the kids! Come quick!"

"Your vandals?" said a confused Officer Scott, sensing Mrs. Rosenman's panic, but unsure of its cause. "Your flowers are okay? Your garbage is intact?"

"It's not *that!*" Mrs. Rosenman said looking at Officer Scott with surprise. "It's the kids next door! One of them is bleeding!"

At the sound of that, Officer Scott was out of the car and at Simcha's side in no time.

"Good thinking," he nodded to Menucha, who was still holding tightly to Simcha's arm to control the bleeding. "Hold on there just another minute while I go get my first aid kit."

"Where are your parents?" he asked when he had returned with gauze to wrap tightly around the wound.

"In China," Menucha said.

"Is that so?" Officer Scott eyed Menucha sharply, thinking she was being disrespectful.

Mrs. Rosenman, who had walked over to where Simcha sat, nodded her head in agreement.

"It's true," said Mrs. Rosenman. "He's gone on business—as usual. That sitter of theirs just went and left them to their own devices, it seems. Now I ask you, what kind of babysitter would leave kids at home, allowing them to walk around in those things? Those skates are terribly dangerous."

"We're not exactly babies," said Menucha, grateful that Mrs. Rosenman had called the policeman but still insistent that she was a responsible teenager.

"No, you're not babies," agreed Officer Scott, cutting off the end of the roll of bandage he had wrapped around Simcha's arm, "but it seems you're not adults either. We can't just hang around waiting for your guardian though. This wound needs stitches. I'd call an ambulance, but for the time it takes for them to get here, I might as well take you over to the emergency room myself. When do you expect your sitter back?"

"I don't know," said a nervous Menucha. "She's out shopping for groceries with my little sister. I don't even know what time she left. We weren't home."

"Four-thirty," was Mrs. Rosenman's prompt reply. "She left at four-thirty."

Officer Scott widened his eyes as did Menucha and Simcha. Mrs. Rosenman really did stay by the window all day!

"Okay, young man," said Officer Scott, hoisting up Simcha in his arms. "Let's go."

"I'm coming, too," said an anxious Menucha, following the officer.

"Sure, come along," said Officer Scott, depositing Simcha in the back seat of his police jeep. "The more the merrier, so long as she doesn't come."

He nodded in Mrs. Rosenman's direction. She was still a few feet away from them. However, Mrs. Rosenman had no intention of coming along. She was too busy eyeing the puddle of blood and broken glass, wondering if Shira would ever get around to cleaning it up, given the low standard of cleanliness Mrs. Rosenman had already noted in the house.

"I'll send a squad car around to inform your guardian when

she gets home," Officer Scott said as he backed out of the drive-way and onto Sobey Road, turning on his flashing lights and heading south towards the hospital. "Though with a neighbor like Mrs. Rosenman, it's not likely I'll need to do even that."

"I'm really sorry about all this," said Simcha weakly.

"That's okay," said a far-from-jovial Officer Scott. "Shuttling kids around because of bumps and scratches, it's all part of my job description. Actually, there's no reason for you to feel bad. It happens all the time. You wouldn't believe how many roller blade accidents there have been this summer. This will proba-bly be the most excitement of my day, probably even a high point of my week. Nothing happens in this dinky little town. None of that cops and robbers stuff you guys have probably read all about."

"No robbers?" said Menucha in disbelief.

"None to speak of," said Officer Scott. "The last time I received a call for armed robbery, the guy was allegedly wearing a gorilla mask and carrying a loaded gun."

"What happened?" asked Simcha, opening his eyes for a moment though not lifting his head from the back of the seat.

"It was a guy wearing a gorilla mask," said Officer Scott, "and carrying a gun, a *toy* gun. He was going to a costume party."

"Give me a break!" moaned Simcha, closing his eyes again.

"That's exactly what I said," Officer Scott nodded in agreement.

"Yeah, well what would you say..." said Menucha, looking over at her pale brother and thinking that there was no such thing as coincidence. They were obviously meant to be here right now, in a police car, having this rather strange conversation.

"What would you say if we told you we had a real crime going on close to us?"

"I'd say," said Officer Scott, "that you should stick to playing house."

"Really?" said Menucha. Was there no adult who would listen to her? Maybe this was her chance to finally speak to someone of authority who would believe her. "Our babysitter is a spy."

"And the guy in the gorilla mask was a bank robber," Officer Scott chuckled bitterly.

"You've got to believe me!" Menucha insisted again. "We have proof. Our father is a major jewelry designer and supplier for the entire East Coast. The babysitter he left us with has been getting into his files and faxing them off somewhere. I have pictures of jewelry she had hidden under her bed along with some of my father's files."

"What were you doing under her bed?" Officer Scott asked, starting to sound interested.

"I was looking for something, anything," Menucha said. "I was trying to find proof of her guilt. Look, you've got to believe me! No one else does, not even my father, or his business partner."

"I'm beginning to believe you," said Officer Scott, as Menucha continued talking, filling him in on everything that had happened thus far, with Simcha occasionally adding his two cents.

Soon they had arrived at the emergency room and, after registering and waiting for ten minutes, Simcha was seen by a doctor. Officer Scott said he'd wait for them outside.

Seventeen stitches later, Shira arrived, sending Menucha to wait outside.

Officer Scott was waiting, leaning on the front of his car. "E-mail me. My address is on my business card. Send me a copy of the pictures you took as soon as you can, and I'll be in touch."

"I can't," Menucha whispered back. "We can only send e-mail to addresses my father approves. It's a special account he has set up for us to keep our e-mail account safe."

"Can't see that I blame him with the Internet being what it is," said Officer Scott. "Fine, what's your schedule tomorrow?"

"I leave for camp at five to nine," said Menucha. "My camp is on Gunar Drive."

"Okey dokey," said Officer Scott. "I'll meet you at the corner in the morning. Bring the file then."

Menucha was elated they finally had found someone who would be on their side, someone of authority, someone who promised he would do something! She went back into the emergency room. Shira, Simcha and Yocheved were on their way out.

"Plexiglas," Shira was muttering to herself while holding a Yocheved who was sucking her thumb and twisting her hair nervously. "We're going to have to replace that window with plexiglas."

Monday night, July 12

"Is supper ready?" Simcha asked, coming into the kitchen with Menucha close behind.

"I don't know," said Yocheved, looking up from the math color-by-number she was doing in her summer homework booklet.

"So, where's Shira?" asked Simcha. "I'm starving."

"That's your fault," said Menucha tartly. "*You* made us late."

"Getting *your* roller blades," Simcha reminded her.

"She's in the garage," Yocheved interrupted.

"In the garage?" said Menucha and Simcha, looking at each other.

"What's she doing in there?" asked Menucha.

"How am I supposed to know?" asked Yocheved, selecting a

red crayon. "Baila Chana doesn't know either. Shira was right in the middle of making supper and then she left. It's awfully messy still, too, so I'm sure she'll be back in soon."

"Are you thinking what I'm thinking?" Menucha whispered to Simcha.

Simcha nodded, and they both tiptoed towards the garage door. They opened the door slowly, trying their best not to make a sound, and peered into the dim garage. They heard Shira before they saw her.

"So, I don't know how well this is all working out," Shira was saying.

"What are you guys doing?" Yocheved asked coming up behind them, her loud tone shattering the silence that the other two had tried so hard to maintain.

"Uh, I have to go," said Shira, looking up and seeing the three children peering at her from the top steps at the garage door leading out of the laundry room. She quickly clicked off her cell phone. "Hi, guys. What's up?"

"What are you doing out here?" Yocheved asked. "Simcha wanted to know."

"Doing?" asked Shira with forced brightness. "Um, doing. Well, I was, actually, I came out here because—" Shira looked around the garage wildly. "Actually, I came out here to find the hedge trimmers. Yeah, the hedges definitely needed to be trimmed. I just noticed that this afternoon."

Shira moved over to the wall to take the electric hedge trimmers down from the wall hook they were hanging on. "When was the last time these bushes were trimmed?"

"I don't know," said Menucha, wondering how Shira could even believe for a second that they couldn't see through her subterfuge.

"Not anytime this summer," said Simcha.

"Well," said Shira with forced brightness. "I think it's high time someone took care of this, and since supper won't be ready for another hour—"

Simcha let out a groan of frustration.

"—I think I'll take care of it right now."

"Tatti doesn't let anyone touch that," said Yocheved.

"That doesn't include me," said Shira briskly.

"I think it includes everyone," said Menucha.

"It's not a problem," said Shira.

"It's dangerous," said Yocheved. "Tatti makes me come in the house when he uses it. He's afraid I'll come too close, and he has to take care of me."

"That's because you were smaller last time he did it," said Shira.

"Can I come outside when you do it then?" asked Yocheved.

"No," said Shira automatically.

"That's because she's not going to be doing it," said Menucha emphatically. "Tatti doesn't let."

"Anything's better than doing all those dishes I have waiting for me in the kitchen!" said Shira, sticking to her guns. "I think I'll do it right now while the blintz loaf I have in the oven bakes, and then we'll eat supper. Those bushes really need to be done. I'll be careful. I promise."

"Famous last words," muttered Menucha. "I'll leave the dishes for you then."

"No problem," said Shira cheerfully. "I'm sure it will feel good to get my hands wet later."

"I'll set the table while you do that," said Simcha, eager to speed up the supper preparations . "Menucha will help me."

"Says who?" Menucha argued, following her brother back into the kitchen.

"Says me," said Simcha. "You do want to eat tonight, don't you?"

"All right," said Menucha begrudgingly. "But who do you think she was talking to on the cell phone?"

"How am I supposed to know?" said Simcha. "One thing is sure, she really wanted to make sure no one could hear. Otherwise she would have talked somewhere in the house, like the living room or her bedroom or something!"

"Yeah," Menucha agreed. "And did you see how fast she hung up when she noticed us there?"

"That's what you do," Yocheved said, "whenever I come in your room and you're on the phone."

"That's different," said Menucha.

"Why?" asked Yocheved.

"Okay," Shira said, poking her head in from the open garage door, "any clue where I can find the plug for this out here?"

"It's in the garage," said Yocheved.

"I already looked everywhere in the garage," said Shira. "Any other ideas?"

"Try looking up," said Menucha.

"I see it now," said Shira. "The garage door plug on the ceiling. Now why didn't I notice something like that?"

Several minutes later, Shira had the extension cord unwound leading outside to the bushes and was ready to go.

"She's starting," announced Yocheved, who was standing with her nose pressed to the kitchen window watching, ready to give a blow-by-blow account of Shira's every move. "She's cutting. She's still cutting. She's stopping. She's rolling back up the extension cord. She's coming inside. She's here."

"All done?" Simcha asked in surprise.

"You missed a bunch," said Yocheved.

"Yup," said Shira with forced cheerfulness. "I know I missed some, but I'm all done."

"What happened?" Menucha asked suspiciously over the ringing of the doorbell.

"I just decided that maybe your father was right after all," said Shira. "I think I'll leave the hedge cutting for him to do."

"I'll get it," said Yocheved, taking Baila Chana along with her.

"Is she okay?" the distinct voice of Mrs. Rosenman could be heard rushing down the hall. "I saw her slice right through that wire, like a knife through butter, and I said to myself, she's a goner for sure. Who's going to watch over the children now? But she got inside all right, didn't she. Where is she?"

"I'm fine," said Shira weakly. "Really, everything's fine."

"What did she slice?" asked Yocheved, rushing over to Shira in alarm and looking her up and down for telltale blood marks.

"The cord," Mrs. Rosenman said, straightening her disheveled flowered housedress, which was snapped unevenly, making it impossible to straighten after all. "I was just looking out my window. My grandkids might be coming. It's such a nice day after all. Anyway, what do I see, but this young woman hacking away at the hedges. First the boy gets hurt and now you. Don't you know how dangerous those things are?"

"I do now," said Shira. "Really, I'm fine. Nothing happened. The trimmer just went dead when I cut its electric cord by mistake instead of the branches."

"Lucky you didn't electrocute yourself is all I can say!" exclaimed Mrs. Rosenman, as she looked down her nose at the unwashed dishes piled in the sink and on the counter. "You would have been safer where the officer was taking you this afternoon, but I suppose they had to let you out to take care of the kids. Maybe you should stick to simpler activities, like washing the dishes."

"Thank you, Mrs. Rosenman," said Shira, escorting her unwanted guest to the door to hurry her along, and pretending not to be insulted by Mrs. Rosenman's insinuation that the officer in her driveway had driven her to jail and not to the emergency room to be with Simcha. "I'll keep that in mind."

"Something really needs to be done about that woman," said Shira, shaking her head ruefully upon her return into the kitchen.

"You weren't out there for longer than one minute," said Simcha in wonderment when Shira collapsed into the nearest kitchen chair.

"Maybe you guys were right," Shira admitted. "I think we should leave the hedge trimming up to your father."

FORTY-SEVEN

"Shira, it's for you," Yocheved said, looking up from the game of Masterpiece that they were all playing in an attempt at getting Simcha's mind off of his throbbing stitches. "It's Mr. Walberg."

"Thanks," said Shira.

"Go somewhere where the kids can't hear you," Ephraim told her as soon as she said hello.

"Okay," she said, walking out of the living room.

"I'll be right back," she told the kids. "Just skip my turn until I get back."

Shira walked into the kitchen where she thought she could speak without being overheard by the kids, who she was sure would stay put in the living room as they continued their game.

"I just wanted you to know," said Ephraim, "that I talked to Binyamin. I told him that I think it's time for him to come home."

"Binyamin's coming home?" Shira asked. "When? Why didn't he tell me?"

"I just spoke with him a little while ago," said Ephraim. "He's really busy there so I don't know for sure, but it sounded like he was going to be able to do it soon, like within the next week or so."

"I don't know if I'm ready to see him yet," Shira said. "I guess a week would give me time, but the kids are acting so suspicious. I don't know how much further I can go with this. It's not working out at all like we planned."

"You've accomplished a lot," Ephraim assured her.

"I may have accomplished a lot," said Shira grimly, "but it's not enough."

"There's still time," said Ephraim. "It's not like he's leaving on the next plane."

"No," said Shira, "I'll just have to work harder, that's all. It hasn't been easy, you know, fooling everyone like this, and then the way the older two have been acting. They're on to something, that's for sure."

"Don't worry about it," said Ephraim. "It will work out, I'm sure of it."

"It has to work out," said Shira. "There's no other way as far as I'm concerned."

"What was all that about?" Menucha asked, as she switched off the walkie talkie that had been in her pocket all day and which had just relayed the entire conversation from the kitchen, at least Shira's side of it.

"I don't know," said Simcha.

"It's not nice to listen in on other people's conversations," said Yocheved, glaring.

"We didn't do it on purpose," said Menucha. "We left the walkie talkie in the kitchen on today when you were gone. I forgot to shut it off. We didn't mean to listen in to Shira. It just happened that way."

"Yeah, right," said Yocheved, reaching for the dice.

"Lucky move," said Menucha, and she wasn't speaking about the roll of the dice.

FORTY-EIGHT

Tuesday morning, July 13

"Here's the file," Menucha said, passing the diskette over to Officer Scott, who—true to his word—was waiting for her at the corner of Sobey and Gunar road.

"I want to show you something," said Officer Scott.

"I only have a few minutes," said Menucha.

"I want you to use this stuff as one final test for your so-called babysitter," Officer Scott explained.

"What is it?" asked Menucha when Officer Scott handed her a white envelope and a pair of disposable gloves.

"Purple powder," he said. "Just sprinkle it inside this manila envelope. Throw out the little white envelope without touching it with your bare hands and leave the big envelope somewhere conspicuous."

"Why?" asked Menucha, picking up the large manila envelope. "It's addressed to my father."

"And marked urgent, private and confidential," Officer Scott chuckled. "We can't get any clearer than that to say "hands off," now can we?"

"So what's the powder in the envelope for?" Menucha asked.

"You bring in the envelope," Officer Scott explained. "You tell your babysitter that someone just dropped it off for your father, and that you were told it was some new designs that were only for him. Look at the flap."

"It's not sealed," Menucha said.

"Right," said Officer Scott. "Before you seal it, you do what I said, put on the gloves, sprinkle the powder in the white envelope inside the manila envelope and seal it. Then see what happens."

"What's going to happen?" Menucha asked.

"If my guess is correct," Officer Scott said, "your babysitter is going to be caught red handed, and I do mean red handed. Ever hear of an exploding dye pack?"

"No," said Menucha, "but it sounds awfully messy."

"An exploding dye pack," lectured Officer Scot, "is something used by banks. Say, some guy comes along to rob a bank. The teller can't do anything but hand over all the money she's got, but she also tucks in a little surprise."

"An exploding dye pack," said Menucha. "But how does it work?"

"It explodes all over the money once the guy thinks he's out free and clear from the bank," said Officer Scott. "It usually marks him pretty well, too, but the money, now that's completely useless. You might as well turn yourself straight into the police rather than trying to use money stained by an exploding dye pack. It's like a red flag that says: I'm a bank robber."

"So what's this?" asked Menucha fingering the white envelope nervously.

"Same principle," said Officer Scott, "but it won't explode. It's just a powder that you'll sprinkle in. She won't notice it, but it will stain her hands red when she touches what we've got inside there."

"So, she'll wash it off," said Menucha.

"It doesn't wash off," said Officer Scott smugly. "I just want to use it for a final litmus test to prove this lady is guilty beyond the shadow of a doubt. Let me know when you start seeing red."

"Thanks," said Menucha. "I think I will have to go home today for an extra snack so that I can drop this off at home to get things moving a little faster."

"That's my girl," said Officer Scott with a wink. "You still have my card with my number and my cell?"

"Right here," said Menucha, patting her blue knapsack. "I wasn't going to leave *that* around."

"Just make sure to leave the envelope around, right where she can see it."

Menucha smiled as she watched Officer Scott pull away from the curb. It felt good to have someone on their side at long last.

FORTY-NINE

It had been a long day for Binyamin. It hadn't started off too well either. He had been bothered all day by the call he had received from Ephraim during the wee hours of the morning. He had tried to push aside everything that Ephraim had said so that he could concentrate on all he had to do during the rest of the day. He had told Ephraim that he would think it over later and now, alone in his hotel room, Ephraim's desperate plea for him to come back assailed him with renewed force.

With a sigh, Binyamin switched on his laptop. He was going to check his e-mails and then check into getting a flight home if need be, but not until he had tied up all the loose ends that still remained. There were not that many loose ends, but enough to keep him in China at the very least for another few days.

"You've got mail," the computer chimed as soon as Binyamin had logged on.

He clicked on his mail, since he was expecting several business e-mails, but first his eyes fell on a different e-mail: EisenbergGang read the return address with a picture icon attached.

Binyamin smiled to himself. The kids must have used Ephraim's digital camera at White Lake on Sunday and sent him pictures of their big day. He clicked on their e-mail first and downloaded the pictures.

With mounting horror, Binyamin took in each picture in turn. Each one was labeled with the time, place and an explanation of what he was seeing, in case he thought his eyes were deceiving him.

Without even bothering to look at any of his other e-mails, Binyamin picked up his cell phone as his panic mounted. He needed a flight out of here, and fast. The kids were playing with fire. Why had he left them with Shira? Given the results, it had obviously been a terrible idea. Now in hindsight, Binyamin couldn't believe he had taken this chance. Everything was spiraling downward. He had trusted Shira! He had expected the same from the kids, or at least he had expected them to show some respect. One thing he had certainly not expected was this.

I can't believe this is happening, he moaned as he held the phone waiting for some English-speaking operator to pick up and find the quickest flight out of China. All my plans—everything—my whole life is going down in ruins. I have to get home!

Twenty minutes later, booked on the next flight out,

Binyamin was feverishly packing. The business interests he had wanted to close up over the next few days now paled in importance to getting home.

FIFTY

"It's a big manila envelope," Shira said into the phone.

"And you say his daughter just brought it inside?" he said.

"She came home from camp in the middle of the day," Shira said. "I think she forgot her lunch again. She left it on his desk, but she told me that someone had dropped it off for her father."

"Isn't there a return address?"

"No, nothing." said Shira.

"I'm sure it has something to do with business, but there's only one way to find out. You're going to have to open it."

"Open it? But it says private and confidential. What if Menucha notices that I opened it? How am I going to explain that?"

"Just open it extremely neatly and seal it again."

"Okay, okay. You're the boss here. I'll open it."

Very gingerly, Shira tugged at the manila envelope flap. It gave with minimal tugging and pulling. Shira reached inside and withdrew the contents, shuffling through page after page of the contents.

"Wait a second," she said in dismay. "It's just a bunch of blank papers!"

"What?"

"I don't know what the big joke is supposed to be," Shira said grimly, "but I'm not laughing."

"Me neither," said her cohort.

"Listen," said Shira. "Why don't I check with Menucha? Maybe she knows the person who dropped this off for her father."

"You can't do that," said the man. "Then she'll know you opened it."

"Oh, you're right," said Shira, shaking her head. "Okay, forget it, for now, but this still seems awfully suspicious to me. I don't know how much more of this I can handle. It's time to just be done with this whole thing!"

"All in due time, Shira. It's almost over! Have some patience!"

"Yeah, I know," said Shira.

She hung up the phone and carefully replaced the papers within the envelope, noticing at the same time that her fingers were covered with some kind of red coloring. Where had that come from? She went to go wash it off, still thinking about the mysterious blank papers in the envelope. She was starting to feel extremely uneasy.

FIFTY-ONE

"Code red," Menucha whispered into the phone when a familiar voice picked up.

"What?" asked the voice.

"It's me, Menucha Eisenberg. She took the bait. Her hands are all red. Now what do we do?"

"I'll handle everything from here on in, kid," said Officer Scott. "Don't you worry about a thing. Just be nice to the lady. It'll be her last night home alone with you guys. Might as well let her enjoy it. Don't do anything to make her suspicious."

"What did he say?" Simcha wanted to know.

"He said we should be nice to her," said Menucha, smiling with satisfaction. It felt gratifying to have her suspicions confirmed.

"Is that all?" asked Simcha.

"No," said Menucha, "but that is what he said."

"Okay," said Simcha with a shrug. "We can handle that, but for how long?"

"Just for tonight," said Menucha. "But, Simcha, I really think things are finally beginning to move in the right direction."

FIFTY-TWO

"This is just too much already," Shira told her reflection in the bathroom where she was trying to no avail to scrub the red dye off of her hands.

"I don't know whose brilliant idea this is, but I have some idea, and boy are they going to pay big time," she muttered fuming as she walked into the laundry room to try some bleach. But she also had no luck with that.

"I'm not going to walk around branded like this," she waved her hands around angrily, spattering drops of bleach all over her favorite skirt, which promptly turned from navy to navy with white spatter marks.

"Yikes! This is too much already," Shira moaned, looking

down at her now-worthless skirt. "If those kids are responsible, I'm going to have to take matters into my own hands, and this means I'll have no choice but to play tough. If that's the way they want to play, then so be it. No more Miss Nice Guy. It's high time I got myself cleared of this mess. It's what needs to be done! I feel like a marked woman like this."

Shira tried a blue ballpoint pen on the bleached parts of her skirt and then a blue permanent marker, but neither shade of blue quite matched the navy of the skirt.

"What on earth are they up to?" she asked, shaking her head in thought as she went upstairs to change. She passed Menucha's bedroom where Simcha and Menucha were sequestered inside. She dared not open the door.

In fact, they were inside whispering urgently while keeping an eye through the window on Yocheved who was on the swing set outside.

Once inside her bedroom, Shira felt her determination harden. "Whatever it is, I'm going to put a stop to it before they go too far with this cloak and dagger stuff. I know just the way to silence them! I'll just have to tell them the truth. Of course, after I'm done, they won't bother another soul again with their silly insinuations, that's for sure! I don't know how the others will feel about this, but I'm going to have to take care of it before Binyamin gets home. That much is obvious."

FIFTY-THREE

Officer Scott hummed as he worked at his desk.

"What's up?" the rookie cop Jamie asked when he passed Officer Scott's desk.

"The sky," answered Officer Scott, laughing loudly at his own poor joke.

Jamie backed off to his own cubicle, giving Officer Scott a quizzical expression; this wasn't the taciturn Officer Scott he usually knew.

"Nope," Officer Scott hummed to himself, "I'm not sharing this baby with anyone. This one is all mine, my very own ticket out of town and up the ladder, that is, if the bird doesn't fly the coop first."

He put his feet up on his desk and leaned back in his chair.

Now, how to best go about netting the biggest case he'd had since he got to this dinky town? No, let's be honest, the biggest case he had ever had in his entire experience as a cop. No wonder he was so excited, he had every right to be. He was going to crack this case wide open, and there would be more than just two kids around to thank him—their father for starters, then Sergeant Williams, his senior officer.

Of course, a case like this would make a big splash across the papers. He could just see the headlines now: *Officer Saves Jewelry Business from Spy Network*. He was not only going to be a hero, he was going to be famous at the same time. Officer Scott couldn't wait.

FIFTY-FOUR

"I think you should take a break from cooking tonight," suggested Menucha, her tone the friendliest it had ever been since Shira's arrival.

"Yeah, let's get take-out food," said Simcha, echoing his sister's friendly tones. "There's a new Chinese take-out place that delivers. All my friends say it's really good, and you could use the break."

"I could?" said Shira in dumbfounded astonishment, lifting the washcloth from off of her forehead where she had put it to try to find some relief from the pounding headache her afternoon upset had brought on. She was lying down on the brown striped couch in the dimly lit family room with all of the curtains drawn, in hopes of getting her headache to fade into oblivion. "I mean, sure I could, but you guys think so, too?"

"Sure, why not?" said Menucha with a nonchalant shrug.

"Don't think we don't notice all that you do for us," said Simcha, with a smirk directed towards Menucha.

"We'll take care of everything," said Menucha. "I'll even do the dishes afterwards. You just sit down right here. I'll get you a good book. Yocheved's up in her room playing, and you don't have to worry about a thing, really."

"Really?" said Shira, in shock at this sudden rush of warm feelings the two Eisenberg eldest seemed to be displaying.

Maybe she had been wrong all along and the antagonistic vibes the kids had exhibited were all her own imagination. Of course, that still didn't explain away the red dye, but she couldn't know for sure that the kids had been behind that. Although the fact that neither of them mentioned her obviously stained red hands made her quite suspicious.

Should she let things slide, or go on with her plan?

"So, can we get it?" Simcha asked.

"Okay," said Shira, "you can order Chinese food, but make sure to get something everyone likes."

"Of course," said Menucha, hurrying off to phone in the supper order.

Shira sat on the couch rubbing her temples. This was too much for her already overtaxed head. Which was it? Had the kids finally come around at last, or were they up to something new? Before the evening was out, she would have to make a decision for certain one way or the other. Shira knew she couldn't afford to gamble the wrong way.

FIFTY-FIVE

Wednesday morning, July 14 — China

Binyamin lay back in his seat, eyes closed, the steady drone of the airplane pulsing through every bone in his body. He was going home. He was going home! He couldn't wait to see the kids, to hear how everything had really gone when he could interrogate them face to face.

Suddenly, his eyes flew open. The kids! He had forgotten to call them in the mad rush. They didn't even know he was coming home! He hadn't had time to charge his cell phone before he left, and now he wanted to conserve the remaining battery, so, instead of using it, he reached over for the airplane telephone near his seat. Phone in hand, he pulled out his credit card, which he promptly swiped. He dialed the number and listened to the rings. After three rings, he hung up. He did not want to leave a message on the machine. He wanted to tell them in person and hear their reaction. He tried a second time in case he hadn't given them time to reach the phone, and then he tried a third time. There was still no answer, which was strange. It would be Tuesday night there, and everyone should have been home from camp already, but that seemed to not be the case. He would try again later.

Later was no different, though. There was still nobody home. Binyamin was left with no choice other than to call Ephraim to pick him up from the airport.

Oh well, he consoled himself. So, they'll be surprised this way, but something didn't sit right with Binyamin. His remaining hours on the plane were filled with anxiety.

Finally, after his almost twenty-hour flight, Binyamin staggered off the plane. By then, he was at a near panic at not being able to reach anyone at his house. He had tried the cell phone he had given Shira numerous times as well, to no avail.

"That's why I gave them the cell phone!" he growled, pounding his fist in his palm in frustration. "So that this wouldn't happen!"

Should he leave right then and there, and worry about his luggage later? If Ephraim would have been there, he would have, but after a quick look around near the luggage turnstile, he realized he would have to wait for Ephraim anyway before he could leave.

Chewing on the inside of his cheek nervously, Binyamin waited for his ride. He couldn't resist one more attempt on his cell phone while he waited. Still no answer.

FIFTY-SIX

Menucha came into the kitchen. They had already started eating the take-out Chinese food but they were all out of cups. Menucha had just gone out to the garage to get a new package from their paper plate storage shelf. The whole meal was being eaten on disposable dishes as per the kids' insistence so that no one would have to do more than the bare minimum of dishes afterwards. She walked into the kitchen to find Shira bending over Simcha, who seemed to be in distress of some sort.

"What's wrong?" Menucha screamed, dropping the package of cups and taking in Simcha's mottled cheeks and his labored breathing. She noticed Shira's hands were still stained red from the dye.

"It's all my fault," Shira moaned, looking up at Menucha, her gaze panicked, her brow beaded with sweat.

"What have you done to him?" Menucha whispered in horror.

"Call Hatzoloh," Simcha gasped between swollen lips.

Yocheved, who had been clutching Baila Chana and sucking her thumb, ran to the phone. She knew every phone in their house came with a sticker with the Hatzoloh phone number on it, though her fingers didn't work quite the way she needed to as they misdialed twice before she punched in the right numbers.

"He ate it," Shira moaned as Menucha helped her brother to lay down on the coach in the next room. "It all happened so fast. It's unbelievable."

"You poisoned him!" screamed Menucha while Yocheved was busy fumbling the dialing. "I went out to the garage, and you poisoned him!"

A cold stab of fear shot through Menucha as she and Shira faced each other. Since Shira had suddenly shown her true colors, what was going to happen to them now?

FIFTY-SEVEN

Wednesday evening, July 14

"Ephraim, hello! How are you? So good to see you! Thanks so much for picking me up." Binyamin put down the luggage he was holding to grip Ephraim's hand warmly. "I'm really anxious to see the kids. Let's go."

"Ready when you are," said Ephraim. "I'll be expecting you bright and early for work tomorrow. Boy, will I be glad to pass the reins back to you. This is no one-man job, that's for sure."

"Not so fast!" said Binyamin. "The way this runaway horse is going, I think we'll both have to hold onto things to slow things down until we're back on regular speed."

"We'll see how you feel after you get home," said Ephraim as the two walked out into the rapidly darkening twilight.

"You can say that again," said Binyamin darkly. "I think this whole thing may have just backfired completely, from what I'm hearing. I sure hope I'm wrong."

"We'll see," said Ephraim uneasily. "Let's just get you home and take it from there."

"It sure feels good to be back," said Binyamin, as the two headed down the Garden State Parkway back to New Hempstead.

"After where you've been," said Ephraim, "I'm sure it does feel good to return home!"

"It was an incredibly successful trip, though," Binyamin said. "I just hope things were equally successful at home."

"That's what we're about to find out," said Ephraim.

The pair drove for the next hour in silence as Binyamin closed his eyes and tried to doze off, but he was too wound up about getting home after being away for what felt like so long.

"Well, here we are," said Ephraim, a touch too heartily. "I'll get the luggage while you—"

But Binyamin was already out of the car and headed for the front door. It was locked. Binyamin rang the bell, two short peals and one long one while fishing for his keys at the same time.

"Hello everyone," he called into the front hall. "I'm home!"

The only answer he got was silence. That was odd. He checked his watch. It was already 9 p.m.

"Anybody home?" Binyamin called again, walking further into the house and calling from the bottom of the stairs.

"They're all in the hospital," said a grim female voice from the still open front door.

"All in the hospital?" Binyamin whirled in shock to take in the wizened face of Mrs. Rosenman. "What are you saying? What's going on? Who's hurt?"

"How should I know?" she said with a shrug, as her eyes darted around the hallway, eagerly drinking in every detail of the rooms she was surveying.

"Mrs. Rosenman," Binyamin stepped towards her. "Please tell me what's going on. Where is my family?"

"I think it's that boy of yours," she said, watching Ephraim as he came in and put Binyamin's luggage down in the front hall. "That woman who was staying here. I heard her tell the ambulance driver last night that it had something to do with allergies, but it could've been some sort of poison."

"Poison!" gasped Binyamin.

"I know what I'm about," said Mrs. Rosenman, her eyes taking in the shocked looks of those around her. "I've been around long enough to see how things go. You leave your kids with a stranger and go gallivanting all over the globe, neglecting your duties. Now what can you expect fr—"

"Ephraim," Binyamin interrupted, rushing past his unwelcome visitor. "Let's go. Now!"

Unconcerned with the wide open front door, or the woman watching him through narrowed eyes, Binyamin ran for the car with Ephraim close at his heels.

"Poison? Allergies? What's going on?" Ephraim asked as he sped away from the house.

"Don't ask questions," said Binyamin. "Just drive and please drive fast. This is my family we're talking about! Who knows what is really going on? She's right though. I should have never left my kids. But I'm sure that whatever happened, it's not Shira's fault."

"You know they were in capable hands!" Ephraim tried to comfort his friend as he pushed the gas pedal down further.

"I knew that, and you knew that," said Binyamin, burying his face in his hands, "but *they* didn't know that. Please drive faster, Ephraim. I *have* to know what's going on."

Ephraim roared down Route 59 towards Good Samaritan Hospital.

FIFTY-EIGHT

Officer Scott smiled grimly as he savored the heat of the chase. At long last he was closing in on something worthwhile. Keeping the case to himself had been one of the best decisions of his career.

He couldn't believe his good luck in having followed his gut feeling. Here was the case that was going to catapult him up the ladder of success. He had it made! And all because of a couple of kids and a rare impulse to be extra nice and drive them to the emergency room himself. See, if people would take the time to listen—but most people didn't. Only Officer Scott had, and the results, well, he knew the results would make him the envy of his department by this time tomorrow.

Room 641, the main desk had told him. He tried to control

his growing impatience as the elevator stopped on every floor along the way to load and unload individuals and groups that all seemed to be moving in slow motion.

"Room 641," he said in an urgent voice. There was a young nurse at the sixth floor nursing station.

"Down this hall," she said, her teddy bear print sleeve pointing in the right direction. "However, that room is really already rather full. I don't know if any more visitors—"

Officer Scott strode down the hall and completely ignored her. He was an officer of the law and had pressing business to attend to.

He stood in the doorway for a split second, savoring the moment—his moment of victory—right before taking action.

Shira sat next to Simcha in his hospital bed. Yocheved was on her lap. She looked up and her eyes met Officer Scott's gloating triumphant ones.

FIFTY-NINE

"Don't look now," said Ephraim three blocks away from the hospital, "but I think we have company."

"Ignore them," said Binyamin in a no-nonsense tone. "It's only another two blocks."

Ephraim pulled into the hospital's emergency room parking lot with a screaming police car right on his tail.

"I'm out of here," Binyamin said, leaping from the car. "You can stay to straighten things out."

"Not so fast," roared Sergeant Williams as he rushed from his car.

"I'm sorry, Officer, but I have to go inside," Binyamin said, totally beside himself by now. "It's my kids, my family! I have to be there with them." And before the policeman could stop him he was gone through the hospital's front doors.

Ephraim approached the sergeant for a hasty conference, inadvertently spilling information that had been hounding him over the past eleven days. Fortunately, Sergeant Williams was used to cutting through garbled accounts and getting to the quick of the matter. Sooner than one might have thought possible, the two men were following fast on the heels of Binyamin.

They caught up with Binyamin at the emergency desk.

"Eisenberg," he was saying for the third time at least as the woman attempted yet again to type the name into her computer database while ignoring the irate glances of the people that Binyamin had pushed aside in an attempt to receive information.

"Could you spell that for me one more time?" she asked, snapping her gum loudly as Binyamin gripped the counter in an attempt to keep from pounding on it with impatience.

"E-I-S . . ."

SIXTY

"Oh, here it is," she said, and then proceeded to blow a huge bubble in triumph.

"Which room?" Binyamin said, his voice choked with impatience as he watched the bubble deflate and sink into her mouth at an agonizingly slow pace.

"Room 641," the woman at the desk said. "The elevator is right over—"

Before the last syllable was out of the woman's mouth, Binyamin was already running for the elevator.

Sergeant Williams and Ephraim got in right before the elevator doors closed behind them.

Once off the elevator, Binyamin headed for the first nursing station.

"I'm here for Eisenberg," he said to the young woman in the teddy bear patterned shirt who was behind the counter.

"More of you?" she said, her eyes widening as she took in the three men before her. "I mean, we really have to limit the number of people we can allow into the room at one time. This is getting completely and totally out of hand—"

She stopped short when Sergeant Williams stepped forward, his eyes narrowing in a menacing manner.

"Right down that hall," she said, pointing the trio in the right direction.

"I don't know why we even bother making up rules," she muttered to herself as she nervously tidied up the files on the counter in front of her. "Why do I let this happen? I don't have to let it happen. I let them walk all over me, day after day. This doesn't have to go on. I *must* take a stand. I *will* take a stand. I've had enough. Seven visitors in one room is just not right!"

With that, the young nurse stalked down the hall towards room 641. She had had enough—officers of the law or no officers of the law. She was going to stand up for her rights as a nurse—the rules of the hospital had to be followed!

SIXTY-ONE

Binyamin hurried down the hall, finding room 641 just as a dark, uniformed shadow disappeared inside. Worry leant further wings to his stride as he stepped up his pace, rushing inside.

"Excuse me," he said to the burly police officer he collided with as he rushed towards the hospital bed. All eyes turned towards Binyamin, the officer momentarily forgotten.

"Tatti!" Menucha shouted as Yocheved hurled herself into her father's arms.

"Simcha!" he said, to the figure in the bed. "Are you okay?"

"I'm okay, Ta," said Simcha, grinning broadly. "It was just an al—"

"If you'll excuse me," said the officer, trying to step around

Binyamin in an attempt at getting closer to his quarry. "Are you Miss Shira Baum?"

The focus of those in the room switched back to the officer as he tried to squeeze through the crowd in the rather confined space towards Shira.

"I am," said Shira, standing up and nervously smoothing her skirt.

"I'm sorry. I must ask you all to leave," said the nurse firmly as she appeared in the doorway, the only place she could see that was left to stand in the room. "This is really against hospital regulations. There are far too many visitors at one time for one patient. I simply can't tolerate it."

"I have a warrant here for your arrest," Officer Scott said, stepping forward, handcuffs gaping, the nurse's statement completely ignored by everyone in the room.

"Oh, no," said Shira.

"Oh, yes," said Menucha, looking on with excitement.

"You can't do this!" Binyamin said.

"This is highly irregular," the nurse tried again. "You must all leave."

"Shira!" another figure somehow managed to burst into the room, wheezing for air as if she had run the whole way.

"Not more of you," the nurse gasped as the newest entrant pushed her aside rather forcefully.

"Mom!" Shira gasped.

"Mrs. Lelchook!" Binyamin said in surprise.

"You know her?" Menucha asked her father, who nodded yes.

"Is everyone okay?" a frantic Mrs. Lelchook said as she

pushed her way through the crowd toward the figure in the bed.

"Bubby!" Yocheved left her father's side just long enough to wrap her arms around Mrs. Lelchook for a quick hug.

"There, there, darling," Mrs. Lelchook disentangled herself gently from Yocheved and approached the bed. "Oh, you poor little chick. Here let me fluff your pillow, make you more comfortable. Nurse! Nurse! Get this boy a drink. He looks a little piqued. You're okay? Shira, you should have called me right away. I would never have known if I hadn't called your house and spoken to that lovely neighbor of yours, Mrs. Rosenman, is it? So nice of her to hold down the fort until you get back."

"I'm sorry, Mom," said Shira weakly. "I was a little tied up."

"And you're not going to be any less tied up soon," Officer Scott blustered. "Now, how about coming with me?"

"Who *is* this man?" Mrs. Lelchook asked through narrowed eyes. "Nurse! What are you doing standing there gaping? This boy's water pitcher needs refilling. Better yet, get him some juice. What are you just standing there for? Are you or are you not here to serve the patient?"

"I really must protest," the nurse said weakly as she backed up a few paces, her eyes dilating in panic.

"Who are all these people?" Mrs. Lelchook asked as she busily folded down Simcha's blanket, "and what on earth is that policeman doing here?"

"She should know," Menucha muttered.

"We'll talk about all this down at the station," Officer Scott soothed his emotionally charged audience. "I and Miss Baum here are going to have a nice long chat about all her carryings on:

her spying against Mr. Eisenberg's business, her abuse of this poor boy, who has visited the hospital twice now in less than a week, and other things like that."

"It's just allergies!" Simcha protested as Mrs. Lelchook and his father turned towards him in alarm. "Really, it wasn't her fault."

"But you'll be leaving?" the nurse tried again, her tone quavering as she took in the handcuffs.

"You're arresting her?" said Binyamin, purposely stepping into Officer Scott's path, "because of *my* business and because of *my* son?"

"That's about the size of it," said Officer Scott smoothly, "if you are Mr. Eisenberg, that is."

"Then I drop all charges," said Binyamin.

"You never pressed charges!" said a shaken Ephraim, who had just come in.

"But you will," said Officer Scott, "when you see the evidence."

"There is no evidence," said Binyamin. "There is no spying. There is no abuse."

"But your daughter and son—"

"—are minors," Ephraim said.

"And my daughter and son were sorely mistaken," said Binyamin grimly. "They'll know that soon enough, and we won't be pressing *any* charges, so you can't arrest her."

"We won't?" said Menucha. "But Tatti, wait until you see—"

"How about we talk about all this down at the station," said Officer Scott, beginning to show signs of worry as he felt something crucial slipping through his fingers.

"How about *you* and I talk about this down at the station?"

232

another voice interrupted Officer Scott. It was Sergeant Williams standing at the doorway right behind Ephraim.

The nurse moaned. "You're disturbing too many other patients. Please, some of you must leave. I insist."

"Sergeant," said Officer Scott, whirling around in surprise. "What are you doing here?"

"I suppose I could ask you the same question," said the sergeant. "Now how about you put away those handcuffs, and you leave this nice family to their own business?"

"But, Sergeant," Officer Scott whined. "I have proof. I have the testimony of these two youngsters. I have pictures. I have a warrant. Look at her hands. They are stained red from the dye in a trap I set up. I know what I'm doing."

"Well, I don't," said the Sergeant pointedly, "even though I am your superior officer, last I checked. You never told me a thing about any of this."

"I can explain everything," said Officer Scott, stepping uncertainly towards his superior officer. "See—"

"Down at the station," said Sergeant Williams firmly. "Now."

"But, Sir," Officer Scott pleaded.

"Are you ignoring a direct command?" Sergeant Williams asked.

"Yes, sir. I mean, no, sir. I was just leaving, sir." Officer Scott turned and looked at Shira. "I'll be back, though, after I have everything all explained and straightened out. You can count on that."

Shira blanched as Officer Scott spoke.

"You can count on nothing, Scott," Sergeant Williams spat at his underling. "Leave! Now!"

"Exactly what I've been saying all along," said the nervous nurse, ringing her hands in exasperation.

Officer Scott slunk from the room.

"Wishing you the best of luck," Sergeant Williams said, giving Binyamin a respectful salute as he left.

"Now that's more like it," the nurse said, brightening considerably. "I suppose I can allow the rest of you to remain if you're perfectly quiet."

No one took heed of the nurse as she slipped from the room still patting herself on the back for her bravery.

See what happens when you just put your foot down? the nurse told herself when she was safely ensconced once again behind the comforting counter of the nursing station. I should take a stand more often.

SIXTY-TWO

"Tatti," said Menucha, looking nervously over at Shira, "You have to listen to me! You don't know what you're doing."

"No! *You* don't know what *you're* doing," said Binyamin. "But first things first. Shira, what's going on? How come you didn't call me? That's why I have the cell phone, remember?"

"We did," said Menucha.

"What?" said Binyamin, taking out his cell phone to check. Sure enough the message light was flashing. "I guess I just didn't check it. I was too worried about not being able to get through to you guys, and I haven't for about two nights now."

"I guess that explains it," said Ephraim.

"So, what's the story?" Binyamin asked.

"Simcha's fine now," said Shira. "We had a bit of a scare. You see, last night the children wanted to order Chinese. I thought it would be fine. None of us thought about Simcha's allergies other than making sure we didn't order the cashew chicken. Now I realize that they must have used peanut oil in the chicken he ate. Oh, Binyamin. I'm so sorry. I can't believe I let this happen. It was so scary for all of us. He just blew up like a balloon. If Hatzoloh hadn't come as fast as they had and gotten us here in record time, why I don't know what would have happened. First he gets into that roller blading accident and now this. It's been so scary! I'm so glad you're here now."

"When is he going to be released?" Binyamin asked.

"We're hoping tomorrow morning," Shira said.

"Fine," said Binyamin. "It's late enough already. How about you guys all go home? I'm staying here with Simcha. Ephraim will bring me home tomorrow morning as soon as they release us."

"Sure thing," said Ephraim.

"But Tatti," said Menucha, "I can't go home with—"

"You *can* go home," said her father in a voice that brooked no argument, "and you *will* go home."

"I'll pretend this whole thing didn't happen," said Shira.

"Well, I can't," said Menucha hotly.

"I think you *can*," said her father, giving his daughter a long look.

"Oh, fine," huffed Menucha.

"That's my girl," said Shira's alleged mother, beaming at Menucha, who only glared back, still confused as to who exactly this woman was.

"I want to stay!" said Yocheved, hurling herself into her father's arms.

"Sweetie, I'll see you in the morning," said Binyamin softly.

"Come, Yocheved," said Shira. "We have a lot to do at home. Remember the welcome home poster we were going to make, and the cake and—"

"Shhh," said Yocheved. "It's supposed to be a surprise!"

"Right," said Shira.

"I didn't hear a thing," said Binyamin.

"Let's go, so we can get it all done," Shira said, taking Yocheved's hand.

"See you all tomorrow," said Simcha.

"Enjoy that comfy bed," said Ephraim, nodding towards the sectional chair that pulled out into a bed for parents to sleep overnight in the hospital with their children.

"Any bed has got to feel fine," said Binyamin, "when you're as tired as I am!"

SIXTY-THREE

"Rise and shine!"

Simcha opened a groggy eye but closed it quickly from the flashlight that was shining directly in his eyes.

"I'm the night nurse, Tabby. Actually, the nurse's assistant," she said, cracking her gum cheerfully, "but we don't have to get that particular now, do we?"

She shined a flashlight across Binyamin's face now as well.

"The patient is over there," Binyamin said hoarsely, wondering why it had to be that only ten minutes ago he had actually fallen asleep in his terribly uncomfortable accommodations. The sectional chair felt like it was digging into his ribs and back at every split of each of its three sections.

"I know that," said the nurse's assistant stiffly. "I am trained to take note of anything that might help with the patients."

"I see," said Binyamin groggily, though he wasn't quite sure why a flashlight shined full in his face was supposed to be helpful in dealing with Simcha.

"Open up," said Tabby cajolingly as she waved the thermometer in front of Simcha's eyes, step one in checking Simcha's vitals.

Binyamin's eyelids closed of their own accord.

"Oops," Tabby said, lowering the flashlight to her shirt pocket, which was covered in dancing, floppy-eared bunnies. "I almost forgot the probe cover, but don't you worry it's—good lord!"

Tabby's shriek of alarm jarred Binyamin fully awake instantly.

"What is that you have growing inside of you?"

She reached for the bedside call button and pushed it frantically three times in rapid succession.

"I didn't see anything about this on your chart," she jabbered, nearly swallowing the wad of gum in her mouth in her excitement. "Open up again, so's I can see. What is that? Could be no one else noticed. This is unbelievable! I've never seen anything like this."

"What on earth is wrong?" Binyamin asked, breaking into a cold sweat and throwing off his hospital white sheet to stand by his son's side and peer down at him nervously. "He looks all right to me. We're supposed to go home in the morning, you know."

"Oh, I don't know about that," said the nurse's assistant, looking around wildly for some backup help to appear.

The ample form of the head night nurse filled the doorway.

"Nurse Jasmine," she said in obvious relief. "You aren't going to believe this. Take a look, just take a look!"

"Calm down, Tabby," said the head nurse, putting a light hand on the other's shoulder. "You're going to wake the whole hospital."

"Just look at this," said Tabby again. "You know I'm trained to notice details and such. Well, it's a good thing, because you just take a look at this here."

"What?" asked Nurse Jasmine, leaning over Simcha as Binyamin did the same.

"Open up," Tabby ordered a shaking Simcha. "There! Right there! Look! You can't miss it!"

She shone the flashlight in Simcha's mouth.

"Look, there at the roof of his mouth," Tabby ordered self-importantly, "and good lord, there's even some of the blue and green gunk down at the bottom. Not even Dr. Wayne noticed this, I bet. There's not a peep about it in this boy's chart. I looked."

"I don't believe it," said Simcha as his mouth snapped shut, while his father threw him a nervous look.

"Open up that mouth, boy," Tabby ordered. "I need a closer look. I'm going to take a swab of it, right, Nurse Jasmine? We'll send it down to the lab and have the results by morning. This is unbelievable. Open up, boy, so I can get my swab inside."

"Sheesh," said a disgusted Simcha as with a gentle click and rotation of his tongue, he opened up again to present the nurse's assistant with one hard plastic, glow-in-the-dark tie-dyed retainer resting on his tongue.

"Good lord!" was all Tabby could gasp before realizing what she was looking at.

Nurse Jasmine was holding her sides as she shook with wordless laughter, and Binyamin had collapsed back on his so-called bed, weak with relief. The adrenaline had been flowing so hard, he wasn't sure he'd ever get to sleep now, but at least there had been nothing new wrong with Simcha. After all, that was the main thing.

SIXTY-FOUR

"So, here we are," said Binyamin, who was greeted at the door by Menucha and Yocheved, neither of whom had gone to camp that day in antici- pation of their father and brother's homecoming from the hospital.

Binyamin seemed, to Menucha at least, to be in an awfully jovial mood for someone who had recently been complaining about not being able to sleep a wink in the hospital the night before.

"I can still feel every fold in that chair," Binyamin had said when he had called that morning to tell them that they were on their way home. "Right down my back here and up at my neck. How can they expect parents to be worth anything if they've slept on that chair night after night?"

"Maybe it's to encourage them to go home," suggested Ephraim, who had been kind enough to bring Binyamin and Simcha home from the hospital and now stood leaning against the front porch railing, grinning at the small crowd that spilled out of the doorway and onto the porch.

"What are they all smiling about?" Menucha whispered to Simcha, after taking in the expressions on Binyamin, Ephraim and Shira's faces.

They all seemed to be grinning ear to ear.

"How should I know?" asked Simcha, turning as Mrs. Lelchook came up the walk and joined them on the front porch.

She, too, Menucha noted, was smiling in a rather silly manner.

"Who invited her?" Menucha nudged her brother, who only shrugged.

"How about we all go sit down in the living room?" Binyamin suggested. "Ephraim, grab my blue bag, will you?"

"Sure thing," said Ephraim, reaching down to tug at the handle of the large navy blue suitcase.

"It's good to be home," Binyamin said as soon as he was settled in the maroon easy chair with Yocheved and Baila Chana on his lap. "That welcome home poster in the front hall was really something special."

"Shira and I made it yesterday," Yocheved said. "It's a good thing you stayed in the hospital yesterday night because otherwise we wouldn't have had time to make it. We didn't know you were coming back from China yet so we had no time to prepare it before. How come you didn't tell us?"

"I didn't know myself until the last minute," said

Binyamin. "But I still brought some things home for all of you."

Menucha's eyes narrowed from where she stood leaning against the doorway. Who exactly was included in her father's "all of you" statement? She studied the faces of everyone in the room: her father, sitting with Yocheved on his lap, Shira and her mother sitting together on the burgundy leather love seat, Ephraim sitting on the matching couch next to Simcha. The light from the front window filtered through the leaves of their spider plant. Its long, narrow green leaves, with the white streak down the middle, were balanced by the wandering Jew plant beside it with its smaller, oval, deep purple on green leaves. Both plants grew well hanging right in front of the big picture window. After plucking off a withered leaf from the wandering Jew, Menucha went to sit down near Simcha. She didn't want to miss any part of her father's homecoming.

"The things I brought are in my suitcase," he explained.

"What did you bring me?" Yocheved asked as she eagerly slid off her father's lap and went to sit expectantly on the maroon, swiss dot patterned carpet, by the suitcase that Ephraim had brought into the room.

"Here," said her father, unzipping the suitcase and reaching inside, "for you."

Yocheved was handed a soft bundle wrapped in tissue paper. Menucha was given a similar package, although hers was a bit bigger.

"It's a kimono," Yocheved squealed in delight, taking in the rich gold threads embroidered into intricate flowery designs all along the hot pink kimono trimmed in black.

"It's beautiful!" said Menucha, tracing the design of a fiery dragon done in the back in green thread along a peacock blue background with golden fire being breathed down either shoulder.

"I thought you would like it!" Binyamin said. "It's real silk, too."

"Can I wear it for my Shabbos robe?" Yocheved asked.

"Of course," said her father. "If you're real careful. Did you know that just one cocoon from a silk worm can be unraveled into two kilometers of thread?"

"How much is that?" asked Yocheved.

"More than a mile," Simcha told her.

"How much is a mile?" Yocheved asked in frustration.

"Oh, from here to your friend Meira's house," Menucha told her.

"Wow," said Yocheved, "all that from one little worm."

"Remarkable, isn't it?" her father agreed. "I didn't forget about your bracelet either, Yocheved."

Her father had noticed her twisting the old gold chain bracelet around on Baila Chana's arm.

"I'll bring it home for you when I go into the office."

"Thanks, Tatti," said Yocheved with a smile, "but Shira helped me make this bracelet, so Baila Chana and I can be twins."

Yocheved held up Baila Chana's other arm and showed her father the zig-zag patterned bracelet in multiple shades of pinks and purples that both she and Baila Chana wore. Several sparkly beads dangled from the knotted strings on both bracelets.

"Those are beautiful," her father said, examining them each in turn. "Now you'll both have two matching bracelets once I bring you home the gold one."

"I don't need another one, Tatti," said Yocheved. "I like this one better anyway. The beads are so pretty, and pink and purple are my favorite colors. Is that okay? You don't mind, do you?"

"Not at all," said her father, trying unsuccessfully to hide his smile. "And you're right; those beads are much prettier than plain gold."

Yocheved couldn't understand why so many people were smiling, but she quickly forgot her puzzlement when her father bent down to get the next package out of his suitcase.

"Now, this is for you, Simcha."

Binyamin held out a white cardboard carton to his son.

"Thanks," said Simcha, taking the carton, which was surprisingly heavy. He opened the box and saw a shiny lacquered box with intricate designs. "Wow! It's amazing."

"It's for you to use as an esrog box," his father explained.

"They sell esrog boxes in China?" Simcha asked.

"I don't think that's exactly what they had in mind when they made it," said Binyamin, tapping the delicate filigree and inlaid work that adorned the top of Simcha's shiny lacquered box, "but I can't think of a better use for it. Filigree and lacquered work like this comes from way back in the Yuan Dynasty."

"Tatti!" said Simcha, not wanting to hear a history lecture.

"Okay," said his father, "suffice it to say, it's an ancient art."

"Let me see!" said Yocheved, leaning over to study the beautiful landscape design of a delicate gold and pearl Chinese pagoda, with a golden tree and several birds of various hues in flight above the whole scene. "I love it. It's gorgeous!"

"I'm glad," said her father.

"It's absolutely a lovely piece," Mrs. Lelchook said as the doorbell rang.

"I'll get it," said Ephraim, who was closest to the door.

"I was out taking a walk anyway," said the grating voice of Mrs. Rosenman, "and I just happened to notice that you folks were home. So, I thought I would pop in and check on how the boy is doing. Just being neighborly, of course. Oh, and I have something that belongs to the little one, too."

Mrs. Rosenman appeared in the doorway, clutching a wrinkled brown grocery bag, and wearing a flowered housedress and her ever-present tattered pink slippers. Her beady eyes took in every article in the room and every person inside of it as well.

"I saw her looking out her window when we all drove up," Simcha whispered to Menucha.

"So nice of you to stop by," said Binyamin, getting to his feet from beside his suitcase. "Simcha is doing fine. They gave him a clean bill of health this morning, and he can go back to camp tomorrow."

"Seems everyone is taking the day off," said Mrs. Rosenman with a sniff, "including the cleaning help."

She looked pointedly over at Shira as she stepped haughtily around the tissue paper and boxes that now littered the living room floor, along with various other items that Binyamin had taken out of his suitcase in his haste to get to the gifts he had brought home.

"You look all right to me, young man," she said peering into Simcha's face. "You gave us all a scare, but it seems as though you've survived. Well, looks like you're having some kind of gathering here, so I'll just be on my way. Never know when those grandchildren might pop in."

"Wait a second, Mrs. Rosenman," said Binyamin. "I have a little something for you here."

"What?" said Mrs. Rosenman suspiciously. "What in the world would you have for *me*?"

"Well," said Binyamin, tugging on a rather bulky, flat box in his suitcase. "Shira suggested this would be just the thing for you."

"Shira?" said Mrs. Rosenman in surprise as her eyes darted to meet Shira's.

"Here it is," said Binyamin with a smile, handing the box over to a confused Mrs. Rosenman, who seemed for once to be at a loss for words.

"Open it!" said Yocheved. "I want to see what's inside!"

With trembling fingers, Mrs. Rosenman complied after first putting down her brown bag. With a sharp intake of breath, she gazed at the contents of her box.

"A Cloisonné enamel dish," Binyamin said in his lecturing tone, "first created during the Ming dynasty but even during the Jingtai period—"

"Ta!" said Simcha to remind his father not to get too carried away.

"It's beautiful," said Mrs. Rosenman with a catch in her voice. "You say, you say that she—"

"Yes," said Binyamin. "Shira thought that a serving platter like this would be just the thing for you to have around for when you have visitors."

"I see," said Mrs. Rosenman, gazing at the glazed vermilion

platter colorfully illustrated with a repeating pattern of plum blossoms and peacocks surrounding a golden phoenix in the center. The handle, as well as the edging, was a shiny gold. "Thank you, Mr. Eisenberg. Thank you!"

Clutching her brown bag as well as the box, she went to sit down on the easy chair Binyamin had vacated earlier, as if this was all too much for her.

"And this is for you, Ephraim," said Binyamin hastily to help diffuse the charged atmosphere of the room.

Binyamin pulled out the largest package in the suitcase— a long, bulky cylinder.

"Rivky will love it," Ephraim said, unrolling a thick Baihua carpet with an intricate pattern of blossoms, prancing unicorns and phoenixes woven on a background of deep cobalt blue. "It will look great with the new couches in the living room."

"That's what I thought," said Binyamin, satisfied that he had chosen well. "Carpets like these were first woven more than two thousand years ago during the Oing Dynasty. Lamas from Tibet came to teach the Chinese how to weave carpets, since they wanted to carpet the entire palace for the first time."

"Llamas?" Yocheved asked, starting to giggle. "Llamas make carpets?"

"Right," said a puzzled Binyamin. "What's so funny about that?"

"Llamas making carpets is funny," Yocheved continued to giggle.

"Not llamas," said Shira. "Lamas are people, not the animals you're thinking of."

"Oh," said Yocheved, while Binyamin shot Shira a grateful glance for interpreting the problem for him.

"And one more thing," said Binyamin. "I almost forgot. Here, Shira this is for you. Actually, you're going to have to share it."

"What is it?" Menucha asked, staring at the cigar-sized box in Shira's hand. It was covered with silk that was embroidered all around the box on every side. An ivory piece, long and narrow, held the box closed as it was buttoned under a loop of the same silk fabric that covered the box.

"It's an awfully pretty box," said Yocheved approvingly.

"Open it!" Binyamin encouraged Shira, who seemed suddenly shy as she held the box in her hand.

"Oooh," said Yocheved, looking inside. "It's so pretty. What is it?"

Inside the box was a tiny ceramic pot that, when opened, revealed a red, clayish substance. Next to it, nestled in the red velvet casing was a heavy piece of jade, carved through and through and on all sides to represent a pagoda. It was about the size of a large salt shaker.

"It's lovely!" Shira said.

"Show them how it works," Binyamin encouraged her.

"What's supposed to work?" Yocheved asked eagerly.

"Simcha, get a piece of paper, please," his father asked.

"Sure," said Simcha, going over to the desk and pulling out a piece of paper from the middle drawer. "Is this okay?"

"Perfect," said his father. "Now, Shira, take the chop."

"What's a chop?" Yocheved asked instantly.

"The carved stone there," her father pointed, "and put the bottom in the red ink paste."

Shira complied.

"Now stamp the paper," Binyamin said.

"I want a turn," Yocheved said, delighted at the stamping kit Shira had been given. "It's got such pretty shapes in the middle."

"It's more than just shapes," Binyamin said. "Menucha, come here. What do you see here?"

Reluctantly, Menucha came over to Shira and studied the design.

Simcha was right behind her as she leaned over the paper that Yocheved was holding up so that Mrs. Lelchook and Ephraim could see. Binyamin moved next to Shira and the two exchanged smiles noted by no one but Mrs. Rosenman, who was too short to see through the small crowd to see what everyone else was looking at.

"It says," Menucha said slowly, barely able to believe her eyes, "it says, *Binyamin and Shira Eisenberg.*"

"And in the middle are the Chinese symbols for happiness, wealth and long life," Binyamin finished for her.

"I think that stamp is beautiful," Mrs. Lelchook gushed with a catch in her voice. "Just beautiful."

"But why?" Menucha whispered, looking wide-eyed from her father to Shira in disbelief.

"That's not even Shira's name, Tatti," said Yocheved, beginning to laugh.

"Not yet," said Binyamin, "but soon, *im yirtzah Hashem*, it's going to be."

"How can Shira's last name be the same as mine?" Yocheved asked without quite understanding, while Menucha's eyes met her brothers.

"They're going to get married, silly," said Simcha to avoid his sister's accusing look.

"Married?" said Mrs. Rosenman in disbelief.

"Married," said Mrs. Lelchook in satisfaction.

"Married!" Menucha exclaimed. "Then Shira's not a spy?"

Menucha was dumbstruck. What a complete fool she had been!

"No. She's a *kallah*," said Ephraim.

"And are you really Shira's mother?" Simcha asked Mrs. Lelchook.

"I really am," said Shira's mother, nodding proudly

"But why is your last name different than Shira's?" Menucha asked, still retaining some of her belligerence.

"How did you know? Oh, forget it, I suppose you have your ways," said Mrs. Lelchook. "My name is different because when Shira and her sisters were about your age, I remarried. My name changed, but not my daughters' names."

"Oh," said Menucha, turning red with embarrassment. She hadn't thought of that.

"You mean I'll have a zaidy, too?" Yocheved shrieked in delight.

"You sure will, *zeeskeit*," said Shira's mother. "I'll take you to meet him this afternoon, that is, if your father gives me permission."

"Do you let, Tatti?" Yocheved asked. "Please say yes! I never had a real live zaidy before."

"Sure you can go," said Binyamin, smiling.

"But I still don't understand," said Menucha, her head whirling in confusion.

"Whatever you want to know, we can explain to you now," her father said gently, sitting down next to her on the couch.

"Well," Menucha said, trying to put her jumbled thoughts into some kind of order. "Why is it that you can tell us now all about Shira, and you didn't want to before? I mean, what would have been so bad to just tell us right from the start who Shira is?"

"I'm afraid that's my fault," said Shira's mother.

"Your fault?" said Simcha, who was suffering from the same confusion his sister was.

"You see," said Mrs. Lelchook, twisting the gold watch on her wrist nervously, "when I got engaged to my present husband, my daughters had a terribly hard time accepting him. Later, they felt they that they would be betraying their real father if they actually liked this man, who they felt was set on replacing him. I'll tell you that they gave him a run for his money. It took years and years for my daughters to appreciate Shmuel for what he is—a warm, loving father.

"I didn't want you children to have to go through the same

quandary. I thought that if I had done it differently all those years ago, the girls would have had an easier time getting along with my Shmuel right from the start. When Shira told me about Binyamin and about you children, I wanted to save you all from the same painful process. I knew you would love my Shira if you could just meet her without the shadow of her being your step-mother hanging over you. So, I'm afraid that all these shenani-gans are completely my fault. I convinced Shira and your father and Ephraim that it would all be for the best, if they would just do things my way. They relied on me because I was the only one with experience in this matter.

"Here they're not even married, and already I'm playing the part of the interfering mother-in-law, something I told myself I would never do. I hope you children can forgive me!"

"But, but," Menucha said, still confused, "what about all those secret phone calls, and the files? Why was Shira looking through Tatti's files, and what about the jewelry and drawings under her bed?"

"What were you doing under my bed?" Shira asked.

"Guys… too many questions," said Binyamin, holding up his hands palms out to stop the onslaught, so that he could at least begin to explain. "Okay, let's begin at the so-called secret phone calls. Shira?"

"Those calls were either to you," Shira explained, "or to Ephraim, who kept calling to check how things were coming along. Or they were to my mother. I tried to make sure the kids didn't see or hear me in case I gave anything away when I talked. I see now that I just made things worse by being so secretive and trying to talk in code so the kids wouldn't understand what I was saying in case they overheard me."

"The files," said Binyamin. "I asked Shira to find the files for me. I needed to review the designs to solidify what I needed to order in China. I gave her the code to unlock the file cabinet, but she couldn't find the files I needed. That's why she kept looking every time you guys said anything that she thought might be important. I really *needed* those files. I still do, as a matter of fact."

"But Tatti—" Yocheved said as she climbed into his lap.

"Hold on, Yocheved," said Binyamin. "I still have to finish answering Menucha's questions. The jewelry and the drawings you found under Shira's bed were there just so you wouldn't find them. The jewelry set I gave to Shira as a present before I left for China."

"It's such a valuable set," Shira explained, "that I was afraid to leave it in my apartment since I was going to be gone for a while."

"There are all kinds of vandals out there," Mrs. Rosenman nodded understandingly.

"So," Shira continued, "I brought it here, but then became nervous once you kids started acting so strange. You were doing so much snooping around—"

"You can say that again," said Mrs. Lelchook, still wondering how the kids had found out that her last name was different from Shira's.

"—and I knew," Shira went on, "that Menucha would recognize the jewelry in an instant as something of Binyamin's, since the design is so distinctive. So I hid it. But now tell me, Menucha, how on earth did you find it?"

"I stayed behind when you went up to the lake," Menucha explained rather shamefacedly. "I wanted to get a good look around your room to prove once and for all that you were spying on Tatti. So, I told the Walbergs that I would be over soon, and gave myself a little time at home alone. Just when I started on your room, your mother came, and I was afraid you might have given her the key to the house, so I hid under the bed. That's when I found the jewelry box and the jewelry designs."

"The designs," said Shira, "were there for the same reason as the jewelry. I was afraid you kids would find it, and I wouldn't be able to explain what I was doing with it."

"What *were* you doing with it?" Simcha asked.

"Shira designs jewelry for your father," said Ephraim. "I suppose we could have told you that much at least, but hindsight is always twenty-twenty they say. Our plan was that you kids wouldn't connect Shira with your father in any way except vaguely that she worked in his office. So I couldn't acknowledge that she was our incredibly talented jewelry designer."

"And *you* knew all the time," Menucha said to Ephraim as everything began to fall in place, piece by piece, including the way Ephraim had avoided her and acted so strange whenever they had met him.

"Oh, I knew all right," said Ephraim, "but I sure wasn't going to be the one to spill the beans. That's why I avoided you like the plague once you began to think you were onto something. It's pretty laughable, now that I think about it, what you guys thought about Shira, but I happen to like working with your father, so I wasn't going to give you any of the answers you were looking for. I'm sorry if you thought I was acting strange. I really wanted to see this plan of theirs work."

"We didn't *think* you were acting strange," said Simcha.

"We knew it," said Menucha.

"I don't even want to know what part you thought I played in all this," said Ephraim.

"Good," said Menucha, "because we don't want to tell you."

Everything made sense now. Menucha felt her cheeks flush scarlet. This whole thing had been a ruse, just like she had suspected, but she had been absolutely wrong about what was going on. Menucha and Simcha could not have been more wrong about Shira. "I don't believe it!" Menucha moaned, noting Simcha's guilty expression as well. "I don't believe it!" she repeated, as slowly a smile began to spread across her face.

"I do," said Yocheved, throwing herself into Shira's arms. "Now you don't have to go away. You can stay here with us forever, and bake chocolate chip brownies and oatmeal cookies, and do projects, and make friendship bracelets, and take us on trips and—"

"Wow!" was all Simcha could say, beginning to grin just like his sisters.

"So, are you ready to forgive me for being a spy?" Shira asked Menucha with a twinkle in her eye.

Menucha suddenly saw Shira in a totally different light. A jewelry designer! Her father was going to get married! Menucha couldn't quite take it all in. How would she ever make it up to Shira? She had been *awful* to her! And Menucha had to admit that Shira had been a pretty good sport. And her poor father had tried so hard to get them to like Shira! Menucha would have to find a way to make it up to her father and to Shira.

"If you're ready to forgive me for spying on you," Menucha said ruefully. "I'm so embarrassed!"

"It's okay. You're definitely forgiven," said Shira with a broad smile. Menucha smiled back with some relief.

Binyamin hesitated, and then spoke. "I think it's only fair that I also apologize. I wanted so much for Shira to be liked by you kids that I thought this would be a good plan. It turned out to be a lousy idea… and I hope you kids will forgive me. I should've trusted you. I should've told you myself what was going on at the very beginning. I really hope I didn't ruin everything and that you'll still accept Shira into the family. What do you say?"

Menucha, Simcha and Yocheved just sat silently for a moment. Their father apologizing? They didn't know what to say. Menucha was the first to speak.

"Tatti! We're so sorry. Of course we'll accept Shira into the family!"

Simcha and Yocheved just nodded numbly.

Binyamin looked on with a proud smile on his face. It looked like things were going to work out after all.

"And last but not least," Binyamin said, changing the subject and taking out the final box from his now nearly empty suitcase, "for our Bubby and Zaidy to be."

"What is it?" Yocheved asked, peering into the box.

"A jade chess set!" Mrs. Lelchook exclaimed as she opened the box with care. "I don't deserve this, not after all of my meddling."

"Well, we think you do," said Binyamin, and everyone in the

room nodded agreement. "The white and black marble chess board is in my other suitcase. This suitcase was already heavy enough. It's a good thing I got all my shopping done earlier in the week, or I would have had to leave without all of these things!"

"This is all so lovely," said Mrs. Lelchook, dabbing at her eyes. "So lovely, and really unnecessary."

"I don't look at it that way," said Binyamin, his eyes straying towards Shira's.

"I still don't get it," said Simcha several minutes later as everyone was talking all at once and listening at the same time, interrupting and talking some more. "What was all that business about a missing file? I mean, if Shira hadn't been poking around like she was, we never would have thought that she was a spy and then this all never would have happened."

"Oh, the file…" said Binyamin. The room suddenly fell silent as if a shadow had taken over it. "It was the file for the new line of jewelry I was going to be producing. Shira designed that line for me."

"So where did the file go?" asked Menucha.

"If we knew that," said Ephraim, "we wouldn't have had all of these problems to start with."

"Right," said Binyamin. "I had the final sketches here at home, and Shira didn't save any of the first drafts, so we're kind of out of luck if we don't find it. I'll look for them now that I'm home, but I can't imagine where they might have gotten to."

"Are you still going to give me whatever jewelry I pick from it?" Yocheved asked, tugging at her father's sleeve. "Because I've already decided what I want."

"When I find the sketches," her father said, stroking her long, dark hair, "you'll still have first pick."

"But I already picked," said Yocheved, ducking out from under her father's hand. "Mrs. Rosenman helped me decide."

"Mrs. Rosenman?" said Shira and Binyamin together as they turned to their elderly neighbor, who was taking in the whole scene in a rather confused fashion.

"They want the pictures back," said Yocheved, going over to Mrs. Rosenman and taking the brown bag from her. "Here."

She thrust the wrinkled brown shopping bag at her father who reached inside and pulled out a leather zipper file.

"How on earth?" Shira said.

"I want this one," said Yocheved, unzipping the file, and pointing to the necklace of choice, a long chain of tiny connecting Magen Davids with tiny seed pearls in the center of each. "I couldn't decide after you left, but I brought it over to Mrs. Rosenman to help me decide and now I know. And I let her have it to look at. This is what I want."

"I can't believe she had it the whole time!" said Shira in disbelief.

"Tatti told me I could pick out what I was getting before he came back," said Yocheved by way of explanation. Her thumb was slowly creeping towards her mouth from nervousness at the strange reaction her news was eliciting.

"Well," said her father as Ephraim and Shira looked at him accusingly, "I didn't think she would take it to mean that she should keep the whole file."

"But I couldn't decide by myself!" Yocheved protested. "Mrs.

Rosenman has such pretty flowers in her yard, I knew she would know what would be pretty for me, so I asked her to help me pick. At first, she thought I was ruining her flowers. But when I told her that I wasn't, she gave me orange tea biscuits and lemonade while she helped me pick some stuff out."

"Oh," said her father, trying to follow the logic of a seven-year-old.

"It wasn't easy to pick something," said Mrs. Rosenman, coming over to glance down at the file. "That jewelry is really pretty. You say you designed it?" She gave Shira a long appraising look.

"Yes," said Shira simply. Mrs. Rosenman nodded slowly and went to sit back down on the couch, where she patted her new tray and looked over again at Shira with a more fond light in her eye.

Yocheved took her thumb out of her mouth as the tension in the room lightened.

"So," said Yocheved, turning the pages in the file her father held. "Can I have this one?"

"That necklace is yours," said her father, "and the matching earrings, too, if that's what you want."

"Okay," said Yocheved. "I'll have to decide if earrings are a good idea. Mrs. Rosenman—"

She reached for the file.

"Oh no, you don't," said her father, swinging the file out of reach. "Next time you touch that file, I'll be right next to you so it doesn't go out of this house. We can decide together, and Mrs. Rosenman, too, if you want. Okay?"

"Okay," said Yocheved with a shrug, "and Baila Chana also?"

"Baila Chana also," said her father.

"And Shira?" said Yocheved.

"Of course Shira," said her father, looking fondly over at his new *kallah*, who smiled back at the pair in return.

SIXTY-FIVE

"**S**hira, do you mind getting the phone?" Binyamin asked from the head of the table.

Shira, who had already gotten up from the table in order to find the soy sauce for the special, welcome home, Chinese, homemade dinner she had prepared the family—without any peanut oil this time—reached for the phone.

"Hello," said Shira pleasantly as she continued to rummage through the cupboard.

"I'd like to speak to Mr. Eisenberg," said the loud and unmistakable tones of none other than the shadchan.

"Binyamin?" Shira said, enjoying the sound of her *chassan's* name on her tongue though her voice grew immediately cold.

263

"I'm afraid he's not available. Can I take a message?"

"I've had just about enough of that," shrilled her counterpart so that once again Shira had to remove the phone from the proximity of her ear or risk damage from the overly loud tone. "I happen to know that he's home."

"And how do you know that?" asked Shira, curious as to how this relative stranger could be so certain.

"I happen to know," hissed the woman, "that he was in shul today for *mincha*. I have my sources and you, young lady, have been giving me the runaround long enough. Now I don't know who you think you are but—"

"I'm Mr. Eisenberg's *kallah*," said Shira calmly, with just a hint of pride.

"What!" the shadchan screeched loud enough so that everyone eating around the kitchen table looked up at the noise emanating from the phone all the way across the kitchen. "You're joking!"

The shadchan suddenly saw all of her carefully plans, hopes and aspirations tumble down to her feet.

"Not at all," said Shira. "Now, if you'll excuse me, I really must go. There are things I have to do."

"Wait!" the woman commanded desperately. "Tell me, tell me something first."

"What is it?" said Shira, suddenly feeling sorry for this woman who had after all only been trying to help.

"Who made this shidduch?"

It was a source of professional pride. She had to know. Was it Elkie Myer, with whom she was in constant competition? That would be a bitter pill indeed to swallow. They had so many of the same clients after all, or had it been Henny Hoffman, new in the field but someone who seemed to have more than her share of good luck in matchmaking.

"Oh, the shadchan," said Shira, looking over and smiling at Binyamin, who was studying her with a quizzical expression. "That would be Ephraim Walberg."

"I've never heard of him," said the confused shadchan.

"No, he's rather new in the field," said Shira, "but he seems to have the right feel for things, a gentle touch but a persuasive nature."

"I see," the shadchan said, even more confused.

"Do you?" said Shira. "Ephraim always says that there's a lot of planning that goes into things like this, you know, but even so, it all boils down to *yad Hashem*."

"Oh, I know…" said the shadchan, thinking of all her carefully laid plans that were now no more than dust and ashes, despite all of her best efforts and fine intentions. "I know."

GLOSSARY

All the words listed in this glossary are Hebrew unless otherwise noted.

baalas midos—a girl with refined character traits

bas tz'nuah—a modest girl

batul—nullified

bubby (Yidd.)—grandmother

chassan—groom

daven (Yidd.)—pray

derech eretz—proper behavior

esrog—citron fruit; one of the four species used on Sukkos

halacha—Jewish law

hamantashen—three-cornered pastry traditionally eaten on Purim

Hatzoloh—Jewish volunteer ambulance organization

im yirtzah Hashem—with G-d's help

iruy kli sheini—lit., "pouring from a secondary vessel;" a process that does not violate the prohibition of cooking on Shabbos

kallah—bride

kasher—make kosher

kli shlishi—a tertiary vessel; putting food into such a vessel would not violate the prohibition of cooking on Shabbos

mamish—really, actually

matzah—unleavened bread, which Jews are required to eat on Pesach

mazel tov—good luck, congratulations

mincha—afternoon prayer service

motzei Shabbos—Saturday night, after Shabbos is over

Pesach—Passover

rav—rabbi

savta—grandmother

shadchan—Jewish matchmaker

shailah—halachic question

shalach manos—gifts of food given on the holiday of Purim

shalosh seudos—third meal of the Sabbath day

sheitel (Yidd.)—wig

shidduch—matrimonial match

shul (Yidd.)—synagogue

tatti (Yidd.)—father

tichel (Yidd.)—scarf used to cover a married woman's hair

yad Hashem—lit., G-d's hand; Divine intervention

zaidy (Yidd.)—grandfather

zeeskeit (Yidd.)—sweety